D0015724

WISHING DAY

ALSO BY LAUREN MYRACLE

Ten

Eleven

Twelve

Thirteen

Thirteen Plus One

The Fashion Disaster That Changed My Life

The Flower Power series

ttyl

ttfn

l8r, g8r

yolo

Peace, Love, and Baby Ducks

Shine

Kissing Kate

The Infinite Moment of Us

LAUREN MYRACLE

WISHING DAY

 KATHERINE TEGEN BOOKS
An Imprint of HarperCollins Publishers

For everyone who believes in magic
(as well as those who may, occasionally,
need a reminder)

And for Randy, my wish come true

I wish to have daughters,
and for my daughters to have daughters,
and their daughters to have daughters,
and their daughters to have daughters.

—NADIA SLOVENSKY, AGE THIRTEEN (1779)

CHAPTER ONE

It was the third night of the third month after Natasha's thirteenth birthday. The moon was full. The winter air was clear and cold. Natasha stood before the ancient willow tree, which towered above her. She was almost close enough to touch its ice-covered branches, but she had yet to take the few remaining steps.

Soon.

Perhaps.

She hadn't yet decided.

Her aunts watched from the edge of the clearing, three or four yards back. They'd hiked up Willow Hill with her, not that she'd asked them to. Not that she'd wanted them to. But when they arrived at the top, they let Natasha approach the willow alone. Also, they stopped bickering. They stopped talking altogether. The silence was a relief, but unnerving now that the moment was here.

Do or don't.

Do or don't.

Do . . . or don't?

Natasha heard the thrum of her pulse. She sensed the rise and fall of her chest. She felt acutely self-conscious. It was like the time in sixth grade when she was changing for PE, and titters broke out, and when she lifted her head, everyone made a show of looking away. Later she learned she was wearing the wrong kind of bra. A "baby" bra.

She was a seventh grader now, and she'd deciphered the rules of being a girl well enough to blend in. But the rules were different when it came to a girl's Wishing Day. Or rather, there were no rules. A girl's Wishing Day might involve a cake, a party, or a special night out at a fancy restaurant. Or a girl might not celebrate her Wishing Day at all. Or she might claim she didn't when really she did, or vice versa.

Most of the girls in Natasha's class did *something* to honor their Wishing Days, Natasha suspected. Even if they didn't come to the willow tree. She imagined candles and ribbons, hopes and dreams scrawled in tiny, cramped letters.

Natasha's best friend, Molly, scoffed at all of it. She was one of the few girls Natasha knew of who absolutely, positively rejected the notion of Wishing Days altogether. To make her point, she'd spent her Wishing Day, which fell in the beginning of December, organizing her sock drawer.

She'd rolled each pair into a tube and set them upright in the drawer. "It makes them happy," she'd told Natasha.

"Ah," Natasha had teased. "So socks can be happy. *Socks*. But the idea of wishes is loony potatoes?"

"Yes," Molly had firmly replied. "Other than Willow Hill, is there any place in the world where girls have Wishing Days? No, because Wishing Days are dumb, no offense to your great-great-whatever-great-grandmother."

"Her name was Nadia," Natasha had murmured.

"No offense to *Nadia*, then. But she made the whole thing up!"

Molly had paused. She'd taken several calming breaths (quite obvious calming breaths, as Molly enjoyed being dramatic). Then she'd smiled. "But I know your own Wishing Day is coming up, so guess what?"

"What?"

"I hereby give you permission to do, on said Wishing Day, whatever you want." She'd swirled her hand through the air. "As it is spoken, so shall it be done!"

"Gee," Natasha had said. "Thanks?"

Molly had given her an *oh, poop on you* scowl. Then she'd laughed and dumped Pixie Dust on Natasha's head, from one of those oversized plastic Pixie Dust tubes. Natasha had tasted sugar in her hair for the rest of the day.

Tonight, Natasha's long hair hung in a braid, which she'd tucked inside her coat. She wore a fuzzy hat, but her ears were still cold. So were her fingers and toes and the tip of her nose. She gazed at the willow tree. Moonlight shone through its branches, cloaking them in a silver swash. Natasha shivered.

"Natasha, make up your mind," Aunt Vera called. "It's freezing out here."

"Vera, shh," chided Aunt Elena. In a louder voice, she said, "Take all the time you need, Natasha. It's your Wishing Day, not ours."

Aunt Vera clucked, and, from the sound of it, Aunt Elena gave her an indignant shove, the sort that sisters never lose the knack for. Aunt Vera and Aunt Elena had very different opinions about the Wishing Day tradition, and they had yet to agree to disagree.

Aunt Elena honestly believed in magic, the way certain children believed in magic. The way Natasha's youngest sister believed. Only Ava was eleven. Aunt Elena was a grown-up.

Natasha's middle sister, Darya, was twelve, but Natasha doubted Darya had *ever* believed in magic. Like Molly, she thought the idea of Wishing Days was ridiculous. But Molly found humor in it, especially the tales of ". . . and it *did* come true! She wished for a kitten on her Wishing Day, and she got one *the very next day*! Except it was a dog, if you're going to be all picky about it, and the girl was just dog-sitting it, and she ended up getting about a zillion nasty flea bites. But still!"

Darya was too cool to joke about Willow Hill's Wishing Day tradition—or maybe too embarrassed, given their family's history. Darya shared Aunt Vera's opinion that superstitions were "the folly of feeble minds." Darya shared other qualities with Aunt Vera as well—good qualities, like being tough when she needed to be.

If Natasha compared the two out loud, however,

Darya would take offense. Darya didn't want to be like Aunt Vera, because Aunt Vera was the *boring* aunt. Aunt Vera believed in properly loaded dishwashers and twice-a-year dental exams for Natasha, Darya, and Ava, whom Aunt Vera, along with Aunt Elena, was raising.

Natasha supposed that Papa was raising them too, but . . .

Well . . .

Papa was Papa, and Mama was gone, so Aunt Vera and Aunt Elena had stepped in.

They were so different from each other, the aunts. Aunt Elena seemed younger than most of the moms in Willow Hill, while Aunt Vera seemed wa-a-a-ay older. If Mama were here, would she be just right, like in *Goldilocks and the Three Bears*?

A wispy memory fluttered at the edge of her thoughts, and Natasha was hit by a deep, familiar ache. She pushed it down.

A nighthawk screeched its short, harsh call, and Natasha looked up, tracking its course by the white bands that slashed through the darker feathers of its wings.

"Natasha!" Aunt Elena called urgently. Natasha heard her approach, the snow crunching beneath her

6

boots. "Natasha, honey, you can't take your time after all. A man who sees a nighthawk on the eve of a full moon should immediately make a wish, for it's sure to come true."

"But I'm a girl," Natasha said. "And don't I get three wishes?"

"But if the nighthawk circles back *before the wish has been made*, then the man, or girl, should abandon all hope for future happiness," Aunt Elena finished, her expression full of worry.

Aunt Vera tromped toward them. "Elena, stop being ridiculous. Natasha, don't listen to a word she says. There's no shame in not making any wishes, you know."

"And yet you made three wishes on your Wishing Day," Aunt Elena said.

"And if I could go back in time, I wouldn't," Aunt Vera retorted. "It's utter nonsense, all of it." Her voice hitched when she said the "nonsense" part. Her eyes darted back and forth.

"Go," Aunt Elena urged, pushing Natasha toward the willow.

Natasha stumbled forward, and a sweet taste filled her mouth.

How odd.

She took a second step. The frosted tip of a branch

lightly grazed her temple, and the sweet taste grew stronger, like maple syrup. Or . . . willow syrup? Was there such a thing as willow syrup?

Natasha hugged her ribs. She would never tell Darya—or Aunt Vera—but deep down, she *did* want to believe in magic. She did want to believe that her family was special, that she was special. Wouldn't it be wonderful if that were true?

The wind skimmed the top of the willow tree, and a smattering of icicles clinked. They sounded like tiny bells. Natasha's heart beat faster, because Mama had worn earrings that jingled like tiny bells. Natasha hadn't thought of those earrings in ages.

Okay, Natasha thought. *Okay, then.*

She ducked her head and pushed through the branches, which closed behind her like a curtain. She touched the willow's great trunk. Her senses tingled, and she heard a faraway tinkling.

(bells, tiny ringing bells)

She caught her breath, because in one great whoosh she knew that magic *did* exist. She felt it in the tree. Otherworldliness burned off it like a light.

Natasha, rumbled the willow, speaking without words.

The world fell away. Her aunts, her sisters. Papa.

The entire town of Willow Hill. Everything faded except Natasha and the willow. No time. No space. Puffs of air floated like small pillows when Natasha breathed; that was all.

She rehearsed the specifics of the tradition:

One impossible wish.

One wish the wisher could make come true herself.

And finally, the deepest wish of her secret heart.

These wishes, if made on a girl's Wishing Day, would come true.

Supposedly.

Natasha felt stuck and more than a little panicky. Should she give in to the pull of the tree, which was strong, or should she walk away now and avoid disappointment?

Disappointment was strong, too. Disappointment hurt.

Keeping her wishes safely contained would be the sensible choice, and Natasha *was* supposed to be sensible. She was the sensible sister, Darya was the pretty sister, and Ava was the goofy, silly, creative sister.

She'd climbed the hill, though. She was here, the moon was full, and tonight's confluence of dates would only happen once. Her palm remained pressed to the tree.

Oh, get on with it, Natasha told herself. *You know you want to make the wishes. You just don't know what to wish* for.

Her list of "impossibles" was endless. To be as beautiful as Darya. Or to be even more beautiful, but not be snobby about it. To do well in school without having to try. To do well in school and not be teased for it. To have more friends. Less responsibility. To not have to act like a grown-up when she was only in seventh grade. To not be needed so much by her aunts and Papa and her sisters—

No, wait!

She didn't mean that. Dreadful girl. Of course Natasha wanted to be needed by her family.

I take it back, she thought. She placed her other hand on the willow and touched her forehead to the cold bark. She let herself go to the dark place inside her, a tender and true place, and spoke before she lost her nerve.

"I wish Mama were still alive," she said, her voice thin and horribly stiff.

Adrenaline made her woozy, and she made her second wish quickly.

"I wish . . . I wish to be kissed," she said, and immediately despised herself. Because what a waste!

10

She didn't care about being kissed. She was supposed to care about such things, because she was thirteen and a girl, and there *were* boys out there who were alarmingly cute. Like Benton Hale. Lately, Natasha had found herself noticing Benton in a new way, different from how she'd thought of him when they were seven and smearing glue on each other.

The pale hairs on the back of his neck, for example. He was on the football team and the wrestling team, and he strode through life with a cocky swagger. Yet those downy strands made him seem vulnerable—and all the more so since surely he didn't know it.

But she wasn't here to think about Benton. She was here to make her third wish. The deepest wish of her secret heart. Natasha's gut clenched. Did she *know* the deepest wish of her secret heart? How was she supposed to know the deepest wish of her secret heart? If it was a secret, how *could* she know?

Be still, child, the willow seemed to say.

Natasha bristled. She was *not* a child. How could she be, given her determination to keep her family from falling apart? She set out the breakfast plates while Aunt Vera cooked eggs and bacon. She helped Ava with her homework. She did the vacuuming before Aunt Elena thought to ask, and she was the one who remembered to buy the vacuum cleaner bags when they ran low. Papa got a rash if his clothes weren't washed with the right brand of detergent, so remembering to buy special detergent was Natasha's job too. And for heaven's sake, Natasha had been the one to replace the furnace filter earlier this winter. The furnace filter! What "child" did that?

The willow hummed. Natasha's grandmother had played beneath it when she was a child, as had her grandmother's grandmother, and it was Natasha's great-grandmother's great-great-great-grandmother who planted it, or so the story went. Natasha was fuzzy on the details. But all the girls in Natasha's family had made their Wishing Day wishes here, as far back as anyone could remember.

Natasha kept her hands against the willow's trunk.

Go back to what matters, said a soft voice inside her. It was her own voice, but not one that rose often to the surface. *Not the kiss, which was dumb. But go to the heart of things.*

You know.

Tears pricked at Natasha's eyes, and for the briefest moment, she let herself feel sorry for herself. She held things together so well. She worked hard and stayed busy and took care of others. She never complained.

"What would we do without you?" Papa often said, laying his hand on her shoulder and smiling his weary smile.

He wasn't really asking. He certainly didn't want an answer. But sometimes Natasha imagined . . . going away. Not disappearing! Well, *maybe* disappearing, but just for a day, so that her absence would force him to see how much he needed her. The same for her sisters and her aunts.

Except, no. That was close, but that wasn't quite it, because it wasn't that they didn't see how much she helped. They did. The problem was that they saw little else.

Likewise, people in town saw how polite she was. Her teachers saw how hardworking she was. Even Molly saw a version of Natasha that wasn't fully fleshed out. Molly was a good friend to Natasha. They had fun together. If Natasha were dangling off a bridge about to fall, Molly would try to save her even if it meant putting herself in danger. Probably.

But every so often, Natasha rammed up against something in Molly that she didn't know what to do with. Like, she wondered how much Molly enjoyed being the best friend of "that poor girl who lost her mother."

Molly was always *fixing* her, for example. She'd adjust Natasha's shirt or tell her to redo her ponytail because there were bumps. She once told Natasha in a loud whisper that she needed to freshen up her deodorant—no offense!

Then, after seeing Natasha's expression, she'd looked stricken. "It's just . . . that's how my mom puts it, when she thinks I smell sweaty. And it totally embarrasses me, but I'd rather know than not know. Wouldn't you?"

Natasha had felt a stab of guilt. She *would* rather know. She didn't want to be the smelly kid! Hearing it out loud totally embarrassed Natasha, too. That was all.

But. Natasha wasn't just "poor Natasha." She wasn't just responsible Natasha or polite Natasha or studious Natasha, either. There was more to her than all of that.

The thoughts and feelings she was grappling with came together with sudden clarity.

Natasha didn't want to disappear. She wanted to be seen.

So. Her third and final wish.

"I wish I were somebody's favorite," she whispered to the tree. "Not everyone's. Just someone's." She stopped breathing. She closed her eyes.

Someone who sees all of me, she added silently.

She opened her eyes and pulled her hands away from the willow. Her cheeks were numb, and she wanted to lick her chapped lips, but she didn't. She knew it would only make them worse.

"Natasha?" she heard. It was Aunt Elena.

"Na*ta*sha!" Aunt Vera called.

Other noises broke into her awareness. Branches rustled. Wood creaked. Somewhere, a dog barked and barked.

Natasha blinked herself back into focus. She studied the trunk of the willow tree, which was lined with infinite cracks and furrows. She tilted her head upward and gazed at the star-slung sky, visible in bits and snatches through the tree's silver branches.

She felt the magic drain away. The willow was just a willow, and Natasha was just Natasha. She felt idiotic.

She pushed through the willow's canopy and stepped into the clearing.

It was done.

CHAPTER TWO

Natasha woke to the sight of her youngest sister, Ava, standing above her and munching wasabi almonds. She shrieked and jerked upright.

"Ava!" she cried. "You can't do that. You're not Boo Radley. It is *creepy* to wake up and see someone staring at you!"

Ava grinned. She had on one of Papa's flannel shirts, which swallowed her whole, and a pair of raggedy jeans that she'd rolled up to the middle of her shins.

"I like being Boo Radley," she said.

"No, you don't, and anyway, you're not allowed to until you read the book," Natasha answered. Boo Radley was a gaunt and hovering character in *To Kill a Mockingbird*, which Natasha knew Ava would love if she gave it half a chance.

But Ava wasn't as much of a reader as Natasha. Neither was their middle sister, Darya. Natasha couldn't wrap her head around it. She would die if she didn't have books. She loved them so much, she wanted to marry them; that's what Darya said.

Ava plopped down on Natasha's bed and drew her legs beneath her, criss-cross applesauce. "So?" she said, bouncing. "What did you wish for? Did any magic happen? What was it like?!"

"Ava. Be still. And also, you have wasabi breath."

Ava leaned forward and huffed on her. Natasha grimaced.

"The moon was so pretty last night," Ava said. "So were the stars. I made a wish too, the 'Star light, star bright' kind. Want to know what I wished? For *your* wishes to come true!"

Natasha felt a stab of love. Ava was so . . . *Ava*. She was sweet and kind and full of joy. She didn't guard her feelings like Natasha, or act loftily amused like Darya.

"That was nice," Natasha said. "Thanks."

Ava popped more almonds into her mouth. "So? Tell me!"

"Did I miss the wish-fest?" Darya said from the door. She strolled to Natasha's bed and perched beside Ava. She smelled good, and her lips were shiny, because Darya was a big fan of lip gloss. She was a fan of makeup in general. She even used an eyelash curler.

Natasha knew that if she tried using an eyelash curler—not that she would; not interested, thanks very much—she'd surely rip out her eyelashes.

What would a person look like without eyelashes? she wondered. A mole? Moles had such a naked look to them, Natasha thought. Same for those wrinkly hairless cats. *Sphynxes*, that's what they were called. Or maybe just *sphynx*? What was the plural for sphynx?

"Throw an almond at her," Darya suggested to Ava. "She's gone into one of her trances."

"I have not," Natasha said. She flinched as an almond pinged her cheek. "Ava, quit."

"She's back! Yay!" Darya said. She took Natasha's hands and widened her eyes with fake earnestness. "Natasha, last night was a big night for you, and we, your sisters, are here to offer our total support. Unless you wished for fake boobs or orange marmalade. In

18

that case, our support will have to be withdrawn."

"I'd still support you," Ava said. "What are fake boobs?"

"Nothing," Natasha said, looking hard at Darya.

"Do you *buy* them?" Ava said. "How do you put them on?"

"They float down from the sky on a parachute," Darya said, lying with her usual ease. She was so good at it, and so *sleek*, that Natasha sometimes wondered if she'd grow up to be a criminal mastermind.

She wouldn't. In her heart, Natasha knew Darya would never be a criminal. But Natasha might write a story about Darya the Criminal Mastermind, just for fun. Natasha loved writing as much as she loved reading, but her sisters didn't know that part. She kept her journal tucked safely away from their busybody eyes.

"Ava, Darya is full of it," Natasha said. "That is not how fake boobs work, you shouldn't even be worrying about boobs, and . . . *argh!*"

Darya smiled a pleased kitty-cat smile. Her skin glowed, and her insanely stunning hair caught the morning light. Unlike Natasha's plain brown hair, Darya's hair was long and red and curly. Soft as rain and shiny as Japanese candy wrappers. At school, she was kind of famous for it.

19

"Anyway, I didn't wish for orange marmalade or . . . that other thing," Natasha said.

"What did you wish for?" Ava asked. "And going to the great willow in the deep dark night—was it spooky or exciting or both? I can't *wait* for my own Wishing Day."

"I can," Darya said.

"I want to be one of the girls whose wishes actually come true," Ava continued. She sought Natasha's gaze. "Do you think I will be?"

"I hope so," Natasha said. If anyone deserved to have her wishes come true, it was Ava. Ava's would be good wishes, too. Like changing the world for the better and all that.

Why didn't Natasha wish for the world to be better? For starvation to go away, for every single war to end, and for everyone to get along?

"My wishes are private," Natasha said.

"Holy cow, you did wish for fake boobs!" Darya exclaimed.

"Um, I didn't, and you're the one who keeps bringing them up. I think *you* want fake boobs."

Darya blushed, which was rare, and which meant that maybe she did. If nothing else, it meant that she noticed boobs and cared about boobs and maybe even worried about boobs—as in, her boobs.

Darya worried about the wrong things, Natasha thought. Like being "hot," a word Natasha detested. It was gross. Seventh graders shouldn't be *hot* or want to *be* hot. Darya also worried about hanging out with the right group of kids, as if kids could be "right" or "wrong" instead of just being themselves.

Suddenly, a hole opened up inside Natasha, filling her with loneliness. She wasn't sure why, but it had something to do with wishing that people could just be kind to each other.

"Darya, you're beautiful," Natasha said.

Darya looked caught out, but she recovered quickly. "Of course I am. Thank you for noticing."

Natasha rolled her eyes.

"Am *I* beautiful?" Ava asked.

"Yes, Ava, you're beautiful too," Natasha said. "But there are so many things that are more important than how you look."

"Was 'being beautiful' one of your wishes?" Ava said.

"No!" Natasha said.

"Good, because you already are," Ava said. She

twined her arms around Natasha's waist and squeezed tight.

"Girls!" Aunt Elena called. "Breakfast! And Darya, did you leave your empty Capri Sun pouch on the counter?"

"No, Aunt Elena, that was Natasha!" Darya said, rising from the bed.

"It was not!" Natasha called.

Ava unpretzeled her legs. "Come on," she said, pulling Natasha out of bed. "You can finish telling us about your Wishing Day while we eat."

"Or not," Natasha said. She grabbed Ava's forearm and held her back until Darya was out of the room. "I'm not trying to be mean, Ava. I just . . . I don't know. It feels strange to talk about it."

Ava cocked her head. She looked scrawny in Papa's shirt.

"Okay," she said. "But . . . was it more than just a normal night?"

There was such hope in Ava's eyes. Would it hurt to let her keep believing in wishes for a little longer?

Natasha thought about how her body had tingled when she first touched the great willow. How she'd felt certain, if only for that moment, that there was more to the world than could ever be explained.

"It was magical," Natasha admitted.

Ava broke into a radiant smile. She hugged Natasha again, pressing her face to Natasha's chest. She felt Ava's lips move against her T-shirt.

"Yay," Natasha heard her whisper.

I wish I believed in wishes.

—MOLLY CARLISLE, AGE THIRTEEN

CHAPTER THREE

O n January fourth, when school started back up,
Molly asked Natasha about her Wishing Day,
too. Natasha and Molly hadn't seen or spoken to each
other during winter break, because Molly's parents
had taken her on an "unplugged" trip to visit Molly's
grandmother. Unplugged meaning no cell phones, no
internet, no anything.

"It was as horrible as it sounds," Molly moaned.
"So catch me up! I want to hear every last detail."

"But you think Wishing Days are dumb," Natasha
said, buffeted by the swirl of kids around her.

"But I don't think you're dumb," Molly said. "I

won't make fun of you, I swear."

Natasha gave her a look. There were certain things she didn't share with Molly. She wasn't sure why. Because it didn't feel safe?

"Oh come on," Molly begged. "Did you close your eyes? Did you think about princes and glass slippers and castles in the sky?"

"Molly. Have you ever known me to think about princes and glass slippers and castles in the sky?"

"Well, princes, anyway. You think about princes *sometimes*."

"We don't have princes in Willow Hill."

"You know what I mean."

The hall buzzed with seventh-grade energy. Guys exchanged fist bumps while girls squealed and hugged as if they'd been apart for months instead of weeks. Kris Wentworth exclaimed about how tan and gorgeous Belinda Berry looked, and Belinda said, "Oh, please." Belinda had gone skiing in Aspen over break. That's why she was tan. She was gorgeous because she just was.

Natasha let the chaos wash over her. A boy named Matt snapped his snow-flecked hat at Belinda and Kris, and Kris squeaked. Benton, Natasha's secret crush, danced for no clear reason in the middle of the hall, fisting his hands and drawing his knees up one after the other. His pants hung too low and his T-shirt was ridiculous, sporting a row of kittens across the front.

But he was ridiculous on purpose. He was confident and cute, and he wore actual cologne. He swaggered when he walked, his hair was a curly blond mess, and his smile made Natasha's stomach flutter when they passed in the hall.

Maybe he was Willow Hill's closest thing to a prince?

Molly poked Natasha's upper arm. "So? Are you going to tell me?"

"Tell you what?"

"About your Wishing Day, crazy pants! Tell-me-tell-me-tell-me, or I will pee right here on the floor, and I am so not kidding."

"Ew," Natasha said.

Molly grinned. She wedged herself between Natasha and her locker and touched Natasha's nose with hers. "If you don't tell me, I will pick you up and carry you over to Benton and drop you in his arms."

Natasha blushed. "Before or after you pee in your pants?"

"My bladder will decide that."

"Tell your bladder it's time for class."

"My bladder thinks class is boring."

"Your bladder doesn't get a vote."

Molly took hold of Natasha's sleeve and lowered her voice. "Did your impossible wish have to do with your mom?"

Natasha shut her locker with a bang. She pointed down the hall and said, "Hey, look. Mr. Parker's bringing new fish for his aquarium."

Molly glanced to the left, where Mr. Parker was making his way carefully to his office with two pet store plastic bags, each filled with water and a goldfish. Mr. Parker was the sixth-grade counselor. He seemed to think that fish made kids calm.

"Fishies!" Molly exclaimed. "I love fishies!" She waved in Mr. Parker's direction. "Hi, little fishies!"

"Didn't your cousin have a kissing fish that ate all the other fish in his aquarium?" Natasha asked.

"Omigosh yes, and it was *so* traumatic," Molly said. She retold the kissing fish story and how, at first, her cousin thought the kissing fish *kissed* the other fishes to death.

"The floating fish skeletons changed his mind about that," Molly said. "So now my cousin has one very fat kissing fish and no others." She walked beside Natasha to their classroom. "Huh. I wonder if the kissing fish regrets his actions, now that he doesn't have any friends left."

Then Molly went off on a tangent about whether or not fish had feelings, and Natasha smiled to herself. She doubted the conversation would double back to Natasha's Wishing Day, which meant that Natasha was off the hook.

Hook zigzagged to *mermaid* in Natasha's mind, and from there to a mermaid *on* a hook. Which was creepy, but could make an awesome story.

When she and Molly got to their desks, she slid her secret journal out of her backpack and jotted down some story notes. Ooo, maybe the *mermaid* could kiss someone to death!

She slapped shut her journal and returned it to her backpack, where it lived during school hours. At home, it lived under her bed, far back in a shadowy corner.

Natasha would revisit her mermaid notes later, and if a story came out of it, it would join the dozens of stories that lived in her journal already. The dozens of *partial* stories, that is. So far, Natasha had failed to ever end a story. It filled her with shame, because she couldn't call herself a writer if she never finished a story, could she?

She could have used her second wish on that! Her

second wish, the wish she, herself, could make come true. Why didn't she wish to write a story with a beginning, a middle, and an end?!

Well, she was *living* her own story, she rationalized. She didn't know what the end was, and hopefully she wouldn't. Not for a long time.

Right now, she was in the middle part, and it was surprisingly interesting.

Not being back at school. That wasn't what she was referring to. Being back at school was fine, but . . . normal. Not the thrill of a lifetime.

Her visit to the old willow had been anything but normal, however. The whiff of otherworldliness she'd experienced clung to her despite the smell of sneakers and the sound of boys' burps and the squeak of marker against whiteboard.

Natasha would always remember the shivery white branches and the magnificent moon. She'd remember how the willow had talked to her, because *it had*. She clung to the memory stubbornly, knowing how she'd sound if she told anyone.

But something extraordinary had happened on that crisp, cold night. Natasha had given the willow her wishes, and in return, the willow had given her a glimpse of a world where anything might happen.

Admittedly, none of Natasha's wishes had come true. (*Had come true* yet, a small voice whispered.) But the *possibility* of wishes had taken root.

Hmm. The tricky part was that this was both good and bad. It was good because it gave her hope that wonderful things awaited her. That maybe she *would* finish a story someday. It was bad for the same reason. Hope lifted you up, but it could just as easily let you down.

⌒

The day stretched on. Natasha answered questions in history and science, though only when she was called on. She solved every problem on the math assessment test Mr. Barnes handed out, but she waited for Rameen Pezeshki to turn his in before turning in hers. It was embarrassing to always hand in assignments first.

On the outside, she acted like her typical self. But every so often, Natasha flashed to the willow tree. Every so often, she heard the flapping of wings. The nighthawk, screeching as it swooped above the clearing.

Her brain felt foggy, and time took on a curious quality, sometimes moving fast and sometimes slow. She couldn't shake the feeling that she was moving through a mirror world—though a mirror of what?

In English, Ms. Woodward told the class to free-write. Everyone else groaned, but Natasha's ribs loosened. She pulled out her secret journal and wrote about her Wishing Day. She hadn't been ready to before, but crossing back into the predictable territory of school gave her the distance she needed.

Wishing for Mama to be alive, she wrote. What was I thinking?

She frowned. Aunt Vera said Natasha would end up with frown lines if she weren't careful, and Aunt Vera would know. Years of frowning had traced multiple fine lines at the corners of Aunt Vera's mouth and across her forehead, so that now she tended to look sour even when she wasn't.

"Why is Aunt Vera mad at me?" Ava sometimes asked.

"She isn't," Natasha would whisper. "That's just her face."

Aunt Elena had wrinkles too, but hers were mainly laugh lines at the outer corners of her eyes.

Mama didn't have wrinkles. Not in Natasha's memory, and not in the framed pictures in the bottom drawer of Papa's dresser. Photos of her mother used to be displayed all over the house: on counters, on shelves, on the mantel above the fireplace. Then, several seasons after Mama went missing, the pictures disappeared. Natasha suspected that Aunt Vera had simply furrowed her brow one day, scooped up the framed pictures, and tucked them out of sight.

Natasha chewed the cap of her pen. She bent her head and wrote,

It's been eight years, but Papa thinks Mama is still alive. He thinks she's "lost" and that one day she'll just show up on our porch. Poof! So I guess he believes in magic. Or amnesia. Or both.

Everyone else thinks she's dead.

I don't know what to think.

There was never a funeral or a coffin or a hole dug deep in the ground. But everyone seems convinced she's dead, and that her death was very very sad and very very tragic because of how much she and Papa loved each other and because of those poor little girls, who are me and Darya and Ava. We're the poor little girls, and when people look at us, that's all they see.

Nobody says how Mama died, though. Not in front of me. Do they think she fell off a cliff? There aren't any cliffs in Willow Hill, and even if there were, there'd still be a body, unless there were wolves and the wolves ate her bones clean. And even if they did, there'd still be bones, wouldn't there? What do people think happened to Mama's bones???

Everyone thinks Papa's crazy for believing that Mama's alive, but guess what? Everyone who thinks that IS JUST AS CRAZY FOR THINKING MAMA JUST DISAPPEARED. PEOPLE DON'T DO THAT. PEOPLE DO NOT DISAPPEAR.

Also, sometimes I think Aunt Elena and Aunt Vera think she's alive too, because of how they look at each other— or deliberately don't look at each other—when anything regarding Mama is mentioned.

So what am I missing???

Maybe everyone doesn't think she's dead. Maybe that's just the show people put on when they're around us.

What, then? Do they think Mama ran off with another man? Except ha, she would never, and that's part of the tragedy: that such an awful thing could happen to a man and woman who were sooooo in love. If you love someone the way Mama loved Papa, you don't leave that person to be with someone else.

Maybe they think Mama committed a crime. Maybe they think she did something so bad that she fled the scene to keep from being put in jail. But, okay, then what was the crime? Why didn't anyone report it?

Also, duh, Mama didn't do bad things. She cut my peanut butter and jelly sandwiches into star shapes! She left gumdrops on the windowsill for fairies! She laughed when

Aunt Vera said she was spoiling us and said, "Life's too short for anything but love," or something else along those lines.

I was a little kid, but I remember. Mama smiled and laughed and tickled me, and taught me to ride a bike, and how to tie my shoes "the big girl way" and not the bunny ears way.

Natasha stopped. A hollow space opened up inside her. Then she pressed her lips together and made herself keep going.

Well, she was sad sometimes. If I'm telling the truth, I have to add that part too.

But no one disappears out of sadness.

So that leaves . . . what?

A nighthawk swooped down and grabbed her with its talons?

A cruel ice queen turned her into stone?

Aunt Vera put a tininess spell on her and made her tiny and put her in her pocket???

I mean. Really. Aunt Vera doesn't even believe in spells.

I don't know what happened to Mama, and I don't think anyone else does, either. What I do know is that Mama couldn't have chosen to disappear, because to disappear on purpose from your husband and your children . . .

Natasha put down her pen. *Not* letting herself think about Mama made her frustrated and unhappy, but letting herself think about Mama did the same thing. It felt like a relief at first, until all that confusion and worry came pouring out, bringing her right back to where she started.

She was dumb to wish for Mama to be alive again. So, so dumb.

A horrid thought struck her. The whole Wishing Day ritual . . . what if its purpose was to teach kids *not* to wish life would magically get better, since it never would?

"All right, everybody, it's time to wrap it up," Ms. Woodward said.

Natasha looked up, disoriented. Around her, kids quit writing. Friends started chatting and gathering their stuff.

Natasha shoved her secret journal into her backpack. She pulled out her English journal with its cheery red cover and flipped to the first blank page.

What a great day! she wrote.

My best friend, Molly, found me before homeroom and gave me an almond croissant, my favorite. I told her about our new puppy which we got for Christmas! My little sister named him UnicornHero.Com, which is just like Ava because she's such a goofball. Basically we call him Hero. He likes my papa the best, and he nips at the leg of Papa's pants until Papa gives in and scratches him behind the ears. Then Hero flops onto his back and holds all four paws up, and Papa laughs and rubs his belly. Papa has a great laugh. His laugh makes everyone else laugh, too. And that's all for now!

That was the sort of stuff a normal girl would write, Natasha thought. She wished they'd gotten a puppy for Christmas. She missed Papa's warm laugh.

She added her notebook to the stack on Ms. Woodward's desk. At the beginning of the year, Ms. Woodward assured the class that their writing notebooks were "a private place to explore their feelings," and she promised not to read their entries.

Natasha thought it was better to be safe than sorry.

CHAPTER FOUR

W illow Hill was a safe and sleepy town. That's
what its residents liked to boast, and Natasha
didn't disagree. Willow Hill seemed separate from the
rest of the world, as if it had been lifted off the broader
landscape and deposited gently on . . . oh, Natasha
didn't know. A cloud?

Which was not to say that Willow Hill was old-
fashioned. Most kids had cell phones (though Natasha
wasn't one of them). There was a movie theater and a
fair number of good restaurants and a cute downtown
shopping area with quirky boutiques.

There wasn't a lot of crime, and when there was, it

consisted of small-scale pranks like cow tipping. (Did cow tipping even count as a crime? Natasha didn't know. She just felt bad for the cows.)

Also, tech-savvy eighth graders constantly found ways to bypass the security controls of the school's computer network. They flipped the school's logo upside down on the homepage. They made the computers type the word "space" each time someone hit the space bar, so that "Life itself is the most wonderful fairy tale" became "Life space itself space . . . ," and so on.

Natasha herself had typed the sentence about life being a fairy tale, quoting Hans Christian Andersen in an essay for her English class. Her favorite part was when "fairy" turned into "space fairy." The image of Tinker Bell twitching her fanny in a space suit made Natasha giggle.

At any rate, most offenses were more aggravating than malicious. There wasn't much malice in Willow Hill, period. In town, people smiled and called out to one another. If your bike got a flat, someone stopped to help you. If you were sick, someone brought you chicken noodle soup. If your mother disappeared into thin air . . .

Well. That was different. If your mother disappeared

into thin air, people didn't know what to do, so it was lucky—for everyone except Natasha and her family—that disappearing mothers weren't the norm.

Still, Willow Hill was safe *most* of the time, for *most* people. The mystery of what happened to Mama was the backdrop to Natasha's life, but day by day, as January folded into February, more immediate concerns fought for her attention.

Valentine's Day, for example.

Girls squealed when they found roses on their desks, or Hershey's Kisses, or teddy bears. Boys turned gruff and embarrassed when notes on scented paper fluttered from their textbooks.

Natasha steered clear of swoony cards and candy hearts that said BE MINE and CRAZY 4 U. She allowed herself to sneak peeks at Benton, but that was all.

In the hall, she bit back a smile when he struck poses while holding a long-stemmed rose between his teeth. During passing period, she saw him get a drink at the water fountain. She liked the way he swiped the back of his hand across his mouth when he was done. In the computer lab, she watched him slap a high-five with his best friend, Stanley. She noticed how the sleeve of his shirt stretched tight around his biceps, and she blushed furiously when Molly caught her staring.

"If you want him to like you, you *miiiight* at some point consider talking to him," Molly teased. "Or write him a letter! Duh! Write Benton a love letter, Natasha. Please please please?"

"Molly, hush," Natasha said.

"And we could slip it into his locker. Wouldn't that be fun?"

"No."

"Okay, then try this: How about you hop up right now, run over to him, and pledge your undying affection?"

"Or try this: How about *you* hop up and run over to him, and then keep running until you reach the football field?"

"The football field? What would I do at the football field?"

"Hmm. Sit alone and think about how not to embarrass your friend?"

Molly tapped her lower lip, contemplating. Then she shook her head. "Nope, that's no good. But here's an idea: Just go over and tell him how hot he is!"

"Ugh," Natasha groaned. "You know how much I hate that word."

"Attractive, then. And *he'll* put his hand over his heart and say, 'Why Natasha, I am honored. You're quite the vixen yourself!'"

Benton and Stanley glanced over at them. So did Mr. Wernsing, the librarian.

"Girls, bring it down a notch," he said, peering over the top of his glasses.

"Yeah, Natasha," Molly scolded. "Bring it down a notch. Sheesh!" To Mr. Wernsing, she said, "Sorry about that. That naughty Natasha is so *naughty*, isn't she?"

"Or perhaps it's the company she keeps?" he said.

"Nope," Molly said. "It's one hundred percent Natasha. She forgot to take her meds this morning."

Then her expression changed. She clutched Natasha's forearm and dropped her voice to an urgent whisper. "Omigosh, Natasha! Benton's looking at you! He's really and truly looking at you!" Her eyes widened. "Whoa. Was *he* one of your wishes? *Did you wish for Benton to like you?*"

Time to be quiet now, Natasha silently and desperately told Molly. *Be quiet, please. Be quiet!*

Benton and Stanley stood and gathered their stuff.

"Bye, boys!" Molly said. "Happy Valentine's Day!" She rattled Natasha's chair. "Don't you want to say 'Happy Valentine's Day,' Natasha?"

What Natasha wanted was to be transported into

another dimension. That didn't happen, so she fixed her eyes on the bulletin board by Mr. Wernsing's desk and tried to look absorbed by the flyers thumbtacked onto it.

"Molly, you're weird," Benton said. "Your friend's weird, Natasha. Did you know that?"

Molly elbowed her, and Natasha startled, pretending to come out of a trance. "Huh? What?"

"Oh, for the love of cheese," Molly said.

Benton grinned. "Adios, ladies. Catch ya on the flip side."

"See you," Stanley said, lifting his hand.

"See you," Natasha said faintly.

As soon as they were gone, Molly squealed. "Benton smiled at you! First he looked at you, then he smiled at you. Did you see?"

"No," Natasha said. "I was very busy looking at the Spring Festival poster."

"Oh, for heaven's sake. You were not."

"I was," Natasha said doggedly. "I was looking at it this whole entire time."

Molly put her hand over Natasha's eyes. "All right, what color is the poster? How many daisies? And is there going to be a maze this year or not?"

"Yellow, lots, and . . ."

"Maze or no maze? One-word answer, babe. Easy-peasy."

Ugh. Natasha tried to peek at the poster, but Molly didn't let her.

"I'm waiting," she singsonged.

Natasha concentrated. The poster had been thumbtacked to the wall since the first day of the new semester, so the yellow background and the explosion of daisies were easy to recall.

But the maze depended on grumpy Mr. Bakkus. How was she supposed to predict what he would do?

All winter long, Mr. Bakkus shaped bricks out of snow and stacked them in an insulated storage shed behind his house. Some years Mr. Bakkus hauled the bricks to City Park and constructed an elaborate maze as his contribution to the town's annual festival. Other years, he didn't. Nobody knew why, although some suggested it was a Groundhog Day sort of thing. If Mr. Bakkus erected his maze, spring would come early to Willow Hill. If he didn't, it could be May before the weather was reliably warm.

The actual festival was in March, and March, in Willow Hill, was invariably chilly.

"Which means they should call it the *Winter* Festival, not the *Spring* Festival," Darya grouched every year. Darya liked things to be black and white. "If it's a spring festival, it should be springy outside."

"But isn't it nice to *dream* about spring, even when winter shows no sign of ending?" Aunt Elena would reply.

"Um, if people want to dream about spring, they should dream about spring. It's not that complicated."

"I'm sure you're right," Aunt Elena would soothe. "Just . . . for some people, it helps to have something to hold on to."

Back to Molly's question. Natasha could feel Molly's warm breath on her neck.

"No maze," Natasha hazarded.

Molly uncovered Natasha's eyes.

"Hey!" Natasha protested. "It doesn't mention the snow maze, period!"

"Yeah, just like you weren't checking out Benton." She grinned smugly.

Natasha *hmmph*ed. She reached over and held down a key on Molly's keyboard, filling the screen with *j*s until Molly laughed and knocked her hand away.

CHAPTER FIVE

At home, Natasha stuck to her regular routine. She roused Darya each day by yanking open Darya's blinds and playing a kids' song called "Happy Bees" repeatedly and loudly, propping her iPod just out of reach on Darya's nightstand. By the time those happy bees buzzed past the irate bull for the fourth time, Darya was awake, out of bed, and groggily threatening to burn Natasha's iPod with fire.

In the evenings, Natasha helped Ava with her homework while Aunt Vera or Aunt Elena made dinner. Ava was eleven, but she was a "young eleven," according to her aunts. Natasha agreed, although every once in a while a subtle shift in Ava's expression made Natasha wonder if she was actually an old soul, a term she'd come across in a book about a boy battling a dark and powerful wizard.

Regardless, Ava was allergic to sitting down and settling in to her schoolwork. She loved math, but hated filling out her Math Mate worksheets. She didn't mind English, and she liked her teacher, who "told good stories." Only instead of reading the day's assignment, she far preferred to jump up from the table and act out her teacher's good stories.

Natasha marveled at Ava's lack of inhibitions. She was quirky on purpose, wearing outfits so mismatched that Darya would pull at her hair and say, "Oh my God, a romper? Really? That romper is giving me cancer, Ava. I am *so* not kidding."

If Natasha had to pick one word to describe Ava, she would say that Ava was a dreamer.

For Darya, picking a one-word description was easy: *pretty*.

For herself?

Ugh.

Aunt Vera would say Natasha "stayed on task," and she'd say it with an approving nod.

Aunt Elena would say that Natasha was dependable,

although she'd probably say it a bit wistfully. She'd stroke Natasha's long hair and tell her that being dependable was great, but that she didn't *always* have to be the one who held the family together.

"You're allowed to do things just for you, just for the joy of it," she might say. She never specified what sorts of things. Maybe she struggled to come up with joyful pursuits Natasha might enjoy?

Papa, if asked to describe his oldest daughter, might look up absentmindedly in his lutemaker's workshop and blink. He'd rest the lute he was crafting on the bench, brush the wood shavings off his shirt, and say, "Sorry, what?"

If he ever did give an answer, it would be along the lines of, "Natasha? She's . . . *Natasha*."

Which was true, and which was perhaps the best answer, if the vaguest. Or rather, it was the best *because* it was the vaguest. Natasha certainly didn't know what word would best describe her. Boring?

Natasha thought about this on the way to school one chilly morning. She walked the half mile on her own, because Darya was always running late and because she enjoyed the time to herself.

But today she was so busy being *boring*, and berating herself for being *boring*, that she ran smack into a tiny old lady standing in front of the sporting goods store.

"Oh!" Natasha said, stumbling backward.

"Indeed!" the woman said, and she winked.

Natasha was unnerved. When someone barreled into you, you didn't respond by winking. Winking made no sense.

Little about the old lady made sense. Not only had she appeared out of nowhere, but she had on the most peculiar outfit Natasha had ever seen—and that included the many creative choices Ava had made over the years.

It was late February, and snow blanketed the town. It would remain snowy for several more weeks at least, and yet the lady Natasha bumped into wore fleecy pink pajama bottoms and bunny slippers. With bunny ears. A bright yellow raincoat was layered over a wool sweater, and topping off the ensemble was a blue silk scarf.

The scarf, which was wrapped around the old lady's shoulders, was beautifully embroidered. It depicted a little girl with a basket looped over her bent elbow. The girl wore a hooded cape and was looking over her shoulder.

Natasha recognized the girl immediately. In

America, she was called Little Red Riding Hood. Natasha's Russian ancestors would have called her Little Red Cap.

Natasha's mother had owned a similar "story" scarf, only hers showed a girl being spirited away by an enormous goose.

"I'm so sorry," Natasha said to the old lady. She had the feeling she knew her, or was supposed to. "Are you all right?"

The old lady wagged her finger. "No, no, no," she chided.

Natasha frowned. *No, no, no* what? No, the old lady wasn't all right?

She looked all right. She looked more than all right. Her cheeks were wrinkled, but rosy, and her eyes gleamed with intelligence.

Then again, her fingernails were ragged and torn, and her hair was a nest of tangled gray fluff. Natasha spotted twigs among the strands. Twigs and leaves and—was that a sparrow? Was a *sparrow* peering at Natasha through the thicket of the old lady's hair?

The sparrow cocked its head and chirped.

Natasha jumped. The old lady laughed, and Natasha grew warm from head to toe.

But *that's* how Natasha knew her. Of course. She

was the Bird Lady, Willow Hill's resident eccentric.

She wasn't just old; she was ancient. No one could remember a time before the Bird Lady. Some said there would never be an *after*. Rumor had it that her impossible wish was to live forever. Others joked that actually, that was the wish she'd made come true herself.

Also, the Bird Lady knew things, things that she shouldn't.

Some blamed the town's birds, accusing them of gathering secrets like seeds and whispering them into the Bird Lady's ear.

Others argued that the Bird Lady turned *into* a bird and did her eavesdropping in that form.

Still others waved their hands at such nonsense. They said the Bird Lady was odd, but harmless. That birds flocked around her because she scattered crumbs for them, that she should eat the food people gave her instead of wasting it, and that if she knew too much about the townspeople's business, it was because the townspeople spoke too freely around her, as if she weren't even there.

Natasha could understand how that might happen. It was as if the Bird Lady had been invisible right up until the moment Natasha bumped into her.

Natasha gathered herself together. "I'm so sorry,"

she said for the second time. "I didn't see you, which was totally my fault."

"Well, yes," the Bird Lady said. "Anyone could see that. Anyone with half a brain, that is."

"Excuse me?"

The Bird Lady cocked her head. The sparrow nesting in the Bird Lady's hair cocked its head.

Natasha, without meaning to, cocked *her* head.

The Bird Lady laughed. "Silly girl. Emily was a silly girl, too."

Emily? Who the heck was Emily?

"There's nothing *wrong* with silly girls," the Bird Lady said. "I, myself, like silly girls, but others just— *poof!*" She fluttered her fingers. "Others forget they ever existed."

Natasha was not a silly girl. She didn't like being called a silly girl. She didn't like being lumped in with silly girls she didn't even know, and she certainly didn't like being *poof*ed away, even by this batty old woman.

The Bird Lady stepped closer than Natasha would have preferred. She smelled like sunflowers, and her expression was full of mischief.

"Forget Emily," she said.

"So I can be like everyone else who forgot her?" Natasha said. "I don't even know who she is, so how can I forget her?" She had never talked back to an adult before, though this felt awfully close to it. Her heart fluttered.

The Bird Lady poked her, hard.

She said, "Ow."

"Serves you right," the Bird Lady said. "Sins of the mother, and so on and so on."

"Whose mother? My mother?" Natasha's temper rose. "*Don't* talk about my mother."

"Sounds to me as though *you're* talking about your mother." She nodded. "I quite liked your mother, you know—though she was a silly girl, too."

"Oka-a-a-y," Natasha said. She had no idea what was going on, and she didn't like it.

The Bird Lady's wrinkled face broke into a wide smile. "Okay! Yes, okay! That's wonderful!"

What was wonderful? The Bird Lady seemed to think that Natasha had agreed to something, but she most definitely hadn't.

Natasha spotted someone inside one of the stores. It was Benton's friend Stanley. He was watching her from the wide window of the sporting goods store his parents owned. He worked there before and after school.

Natasha was mortified. She knew Stanley couldn't

have overheard her conversation with the Bird Lady. But he'd seen them together. He'd seen them talking.

"Girls are *all* so silly," the Bird Lady said. "Don't you agree, pet?"

Natasha sidled around the Bird Lady and hurried toward school. Behind her, she heard the concurring chirp of the Bird Lady's sparrow.

CHAPTER SIX

"What's wrong?" Molly asked Natasha at her locker. "You look like you saw a ghost."

Natasha clamped her lips together.

"For real," Molly said. She tapped Natasha's shoulder, in the exact same spot where the Bird Lady had.

The Bird Lady had touched her, and said weird things to her, and then she'd *laughed* at her.

Silly, silly girl. No, *silly, silly girls.* Plural, because of Emily, whoever that was, and Natasha's mother, whom the Bird Lady had "quite liked."

Natasha had prickled when the Bird Lady mentioned Mama. The Bird Lady wasn't allowed to mention Mama, whether she'd liked her or not. There should be a law against it.

"Natasha," Molly said in a singsong voice. "I will pester you until you tell me, so you might as well get it over with." She widened her eyes. "Ooo! *Did* you see a ghost? I will be so jealous if you saw a ghost. Not that I believe in ghosts. But did you?"

A boy shut his locker with a bang. Natasha flinched.

Molly studied her. In a gentler tone, she asked, "Hey, are you all right?"

"Do you know anyone named Emily?" Natasha blurted.

"No. Why?"

"No reason."

"Liar."

Natasha dug her fingernails into the pad of her palm. "Something strange happened on the way to school, but it's not important. Anyway, I probably made it up."

Over the next four hours, Natasha wondered if she *had* made up her encounter with the Bird Lady. If there was *any possible way* she'd imagined it all.

But she hadn't. She knew she hadn't.

When noon arrived, she and Molly claimed their

usual table at the back of the cafeteria. One other person sat with them, only not really, since he chose the farthest-away seat. Also, he had his nose in a book. He wore earbuds, and whatever he was listening to was turned up loudly enough for Natasha to hear it. It sounded like the soundtrack to a video game.

Fifteen feet away, in the middle of the room, Natasha's sister Darya held court among her friends. Thanks to the age cutoffs dictated by the school calendar, Natasha and Darya were both in the seventh grade. They stuck to their own circles pretty much, though. Or, Darya stuck to her circle. Natasha hung out with Molly.

"You don't have to let her outshine you, you know," Molly said, gesturing at Darya. Darya's red curls bounced as she laughed. Girls clamored for her attention. She *was* extremely shiny.

"Who said I was?" Natasha said.

"If you curled your hair, and maybe used some shine serum, and wore skirts more often—"

"Thanks for your input," Natasha said shortly. "I'm fine with who I am, actually."

Molly hit her forehead with the heel of her palm. "*Bad* Molly! Bad!" She touched Natasha's arm. "Sorry. I didn't mean it in a judgy way."

Natasha wanted to twitch away Molly's hand. She didn't, because then Molly would apologize a hundred *more* times. Then she'd try to psychoanalyze Natasha to find out why talking about Darya was so hard, and she'd be anxious and concerned, and it would all be for nothing because Natasha had no problem talking about Darya!

She didn't want to *be* Darya, that's all.

And she didn't want to be mothered or babied or "fixed," not by Molly.

Molly started to say something, but didn't. Instead she slurped her mixed-berry smoothie, which came in a squeezable plastic pouch and was actually baby food. On the front of the pouch was a picture of Grover from *Sesame Street* holding an armful of strawberries and blueberries. On the back of the pouch, it said, "I, your furry friend Grover, adore delicious mixed berries!"

Maybe it was Molly who wanted to get all sorts of attention, like Darya. Maybe packing baby food in her lunch was her way of showing off?

Maybe Molly's the one who needs psychoanalyzing, Natasha thought, and she felt better.

"So tell me about this morning," Molly prompted, propping her elbow on the table and resting her chin on her palm. "What was the strange thing that happened?"

Natasha felt reluctance build up inside her, like wet sand. "Huh? Oh. I don't even remember."

"Yes, you do. You were freaked out, I could totally tell."

Natasha sighed. Then she gave Molly an abbreviated account of the morning's events. In her shortened version, she didn't physically run into the Bird Lady, and she didn't have a conversation with her. She simply saw her, nothing more.

"And there was a *bird* in her hair?" Molly said, delighted. "A living, breathing bird?"

She giggled, and Natasha felt annoyed. The thought rose in her head that *Molly* was a silly girl, *a silly, silly girl*. But the words didn't feel like her own, and a shiver rippled down her spine.

"Anyway, that's the whole story," Natasha said. "I saw the Bird Lady. She was weird. The end."

"She's probably lonely," Molly mused. "If you see her again, you should, like, try to get to know her. Just because she's crazy doesn't mean she doesn't need friends."

"You shouldn't say 'crazy.'"

"Mentally ill, whatever." Molly shrugged. "Maybe she's manic-depressive. Maybe today you saw her manic side, and next time you'll see her depressed side."

Natasha flattened her hands on the cafeteria table. Mama had had a depressed side. *Her dark times*, that's how Mama had described the days when she didn't get out of bed. Natasha hated thinking of Mama descending into darkness. She even hated thinking of the Bird Lady descending into darkness. She didn't want that for anyone.

"My cousin, Lucille?" Molly said. "Who lives in the apartment complex near the railroad tracks? She knew a woman who was *always* depressed. Also she had hair everywhere, including her arms and hands and even her palms." She paused. "I don't think the hair was related to her depression, though."

Natasha had no reply. Molly said the most bizarre things, usually in a completely offhand way. *My mom baked blueberry muffins for breakfast, with real blueberries. Not canned. And Lucille? My cousin? She knows a very hairy woman who happens to be depressed.* (Beat.) *Hey, do you have any lip gloss?*

Movement drew Natasha's attention. She looked up and saw a bird swoop from one end of the cafeteria to the other. She blinked, shook her head, and looked again.

"Molly?" she said. She pointed. "There's a bird in the cafeteria."

Molly's mouth fell open. Then she grinned and said, "Awww! Hi, little birdie!" To Natasha, she said, "Is that the same bird you saw in the Bird Lady's hair?"

"The Bird Lady's bird was brown."

"This one's blue, so not the same. But why is there a bluebird in the cafeteria?"

"I have no idea."

"Maybe he's hungry. Maybe he needs some bread crumbs." Molly scanned the table. The earbud boy sitting across from them had a sandwich, and Molly leaned over and picked up the part he hadn't yet eaten.

"Hey!" he said.

She pulled off the crust and tossed the rest back. She tore the crust into smaller bits and sprinkled them on the floor. "Here, little birdie! Food! See?"

The bird made another pass across the room. It dipped low and hovered in front of the cafeteria's wide glass window, and Natasha felt faint. Outside the lunchroom, partially obscured by the thicket of trees bordering the courtyard, was a person.

A lady.

A tiny lady in a yellow raincoat and bunny slippers who was doing a terrible job of being sneaky, if being sneaky was her goal. She popped out from behind a snow-covered pine and waved her scarf back and forth, like a matador trying to attract a bull. Then she ducked back behind the tree. She popped out again, her smile lighting up her face. She waved the scarf wildly. Then, far too nimbly for someone so old, she darted once more behind the tree.

No, Natasha thought. The Bird Lady could not be outside the cafeteria, during lunch, waving at Natasha while everyone else ate and chatted and squirted too much ketchup over their fries. Nor could she be swishing her Little Red Cap scarf back and forth, the silk rippling and fluttering like something alive.

Except she was, and that particular kind of story scarf was called a *mantilla*. Natasha just remembered.

"Molly?" Natasha said. "Do you see that lady out there?"

The Bird Lady did a strange foot-hopping dance, waving her mantilla back and forth.

"The birdie's not eating the bread crumbs," Molly complained. "Eat the bread crumbs, birdie!"

Natasha twisted in her seat, searching for Darya. If Darya was looking out the window . . . if Darya saw the Bird Lady . . .

Would that make things better or worse?

Darya was hunched together with two other girls,

the three of them laughing at something on one of the girls' phone.

It started snowing. The scrim of white made Natasha even more dizzy. The Bird Lady beckoned her, using her hand to say, *Come along, hurry now, quick-quick-quick*. Natasha half rose from her chair, and if Molly hadn't yanked her back, she didn't know what she would have done.

"What are you doing?" Molly said. "You've eaten, like, one bite of your apple." She thrust out her squeezable plastic pouch with Grover on the front. "Here, take this."

Natasha grabbed Molly's wrist. Molly's eyes widened. "Look out the window. The Bird Lady's right there!"

Molly turned and squinted through the glass. Snow fell thickly from the gray sky. The old lady was gone.

"You are so random, Natasha," Molly said. "First you say there's a bird in the cafeteria, only ha ha, not really. Then, 'Look, there's an old lady!', only not really again. And then you completely zoned out, like you weren't even here."

"There *was* an old lady," Natasha said.

"Yeah, this morning on your way to school," Molly

said. She took a sip of her *Sesame Street* smoothie.

"And the bird—you saw the bird!" Natasha cried. "You *fed* the bird!" She gestured at the floor beneath Molly's chair, where Molly had dropped the bread crumbs.

They weren't there.

She glanced up and around the cafeteria ceiling.

No bird. Not even a feather.

"Natasha?" Molly said.

Natasha looked out the window. Then she looked at Earbud Boy, who held a graphic novel in one hand and his sandwich in the other. There were bite marks on the sandwich, but no missing strip of crust.

The little hairs on the back of Natasha's neck stood up.

It was as if the real world had collided with a hidden world, a world which other people couldn't see. Possible and impossible, tangled hopelessly together.

*I wish to be in charge of something,
so I can boss people around
and they'll have to listen.*

—Vera Kovrov, age thirteen

CHAPTER SEVEN

Natasha stayed on high alert for the next several days, waiting for more odd things to happen. When nothing did, she felt curiously let down.

Then, four days after her encounter with the Bird Lady, she overheard her aunts talking about her. It was Tuesday morning, and Natasha was heading downstairs for breakfast. She froze.

". . . but what *you* don't seem to understand is that I want what's best for her too," Aunt Vera was saying. "Natasha was *five years old* when Klara left. Five years old!"

"Yes, Vera," Aunt Elena said. "I was there, too."

"She'd started kindergarten only days before, and afterward, for weeks, she said, 'Why isn't Mama taking me? Why can't Mama pack my lunch?'"

"It broke my heart," Aunt Elena said.

"*Klara* broke her heart," Aunt Vera said. There was an edge to her voice. "Klara broke everyone's hearts."

"Vera, please. I'm not trying to rewrite history," Aunt Elena said. "I just . . . I don't want you to *erase* history."

"The past belongs in the past," Aunt Vera said. "I told you that on Natasha's Wishing Day. I told you nothing good would come of it."

"How do we know nothing good came of it? How do we know if anything happened at all, since we don't know what she wished for?"

"Elena, leave it alone," Aunt Vera said.

Aunt Elena lowered her voice, and Natasha strained to hear. "Klara never told me her wishes, either. Did she tell you?"

Silence.

"The girls used to ask. They asked what our wishes were and what their mother's wishes had been," Aunt Elena said.

"Not Darya."

"Yes, even Darya. They adored talking about

Wishing Day—until they learned not to."

"*Learned* not to. Exactly," Aunt Vera said. "You say it as if I did something bad, but I did it to help them."

"Why did you go with us to the top of Willow Hill, on Natasha's Wishing Day?" Aunt Elena asked.

"Because . . . well, because . . ."

"Because one thing we *do* know is that Klara believed in Wishing Day magic. Klara wanted the tradition to live on."

"One moment she did, one moment she didn't," Aunt Vera said. "That's how I recall it."

"And the tradition *has* lived on," Aunt Elena said. "Every girl in Willow Hill knows about it. Every boy, too, I suspect. If we had let Natasha's Wishing Day simply pass by, what message would that have sent?"

"Enough, Elena," Aunt Vera snapped. "Encouraging children to believe in magic does nothing but cause pain."

"That's not true."

"Isn't it? Natasha hardly touched her dinner last night. She went straight to her room at eight o'clock, but the light under her door was on until almost eleven."

"She's a teenager," Aunt Elena said. "Teenagers are moody."

"Klara was moody," Aunt Vera challenged. "For that matter, Klara's moodiness started right after *her* Wishing Day. So there!"

Natasha frowned. *Was* she moody, like Mama? She tromped down the remaining stairs, and Aunt Elena smoothly changed the subject. "What we need is *khrenovina* sauce, don't you think?"

"And sour cream," Aunt Vera said. Then, "Good morning, Natasha. Aunt Elena's making her *pelmeni* for us. Fried *pelmeni* with *khrenovina* sauce, now that's a dinner fit for a cold night."

"And maybe I'll make honey cookies for dessert," Aunt Elena said. She turned off the stove and moved the eggs from the heat. "Your mother made the most delicious honey cookies, Natasha."

Natasha took a seat at the table. Feet thumped on the stairs, and Ava burst into the kitchen, a whirlwind of messy braids, socks-turned-into-arm-warmers, and a shirt of Papa's that she'd modified by bunching up the excess fabric and securing it with a rubber band.

"Honey cookies?" she sang. "Did I hear someone say ho-o-o-o-ney cookies?" She grinned and twirled. "You made at least twenty-five, right, Aunt Elena? If we bring a food item, the rule is it has to be enough for everyone."

Aunt Elena's eyes widened. "Oh, no. Ava, sweetie . . ."

"For our unit on family histories. For my presentation."

"I thought I'd make them tonight, for the family. I forgot about your presentation!"

Ava's smile faltered. "You for*got?*"

"Not entirely! They were on my mind, clearly! I forgot *why* I kept thinking about them, that's all!"

A new noise came from the staircase: the precise clop-clop of Darya's one-inch heels. "One inch" because that was as high as the aunts allowed; "heels" because Darya was Darya and refused to wear snow boots. She thought they were ugly.

"Uh-oh, no cookies for your presentation?" she said. She tightened her ponytail, which hung in a bouncy spiral. "Oh well. Guess you'll fail."

"Darya!" the aunts said.

Darya laced her fingers and stretched, straightening her arms and reaching her upturned palms toward the ceiling. She was slender and strong and graceful, the type of girl who would never run smack into a tiny old lady with a bird in her hair. Who would never *believe* in a tiny old lady with a bird in her hair.

Natasha thought about the conversation she'd overheard, and Aunt Elena's claim that "even Darya" used to adore talking about Wishing Days. Maybe or maybe not, but that Darya no longer existed.

"What am I going to do?" Ava wailed. "My presentation is *today*. My teacher is going to hate me!"

"Ava, slow down," said Aunt Vera. "It's not the end of the world."

"Yeah-huh, because I *have* to bring a cultural artifact. It's the biggest part of the assignment. Fred Williams had Bulgaria—"

"*Fred*?" Darya said. "Who names their kid Fred?"

"And he dressed up as Viktor Krum. He wore a red robe and carried a flag and everything!"

Darya held open her hands. "Who the heck is Viktor Krum, and what does he have to do with anything?"

"He was on the Bulgarian Quidditch team," Natasha explained. "From Harry Potter." She turned to Ava. "And Ava, you were supposed to *help* Aunt Elena make the cookies. If you're going to blame anyone, blame yourself."

"Wait," Darya said. "If that dude was from Harry Potter, then he's not real. He's made up."

"Ms. Gupta said it was okay," Ava said. "Plus Fred gave facts about the real Bulgaria."

"As I am not interested in this conversation, I am

going to go fold laundry," Aunt Vera said, untying her apron and laying it on the counter.

"I'll help," Aunt Elena said.

"You scared them away," Darya said. "You made them feel like bad parents."

"They're *not* parents," Ava said.

"You could have brought one of them as your artifact. They're Russian, kind of." Darya tsk-ed. "But you blew that opportunity, didn't you? And made our dear sweet aunts feel like crap, all in one fell swoop."

Ava's eyes widened. Tears welled and threatened to spill over.

"*Darya,*" Natasha said.

"What?" Darya said.

Natasha gave her a look, and Darya's smile fell away. Her teasing hadn't been funny; she'd made Ava feel bad, she'd gone too far. All of this played across Darya's face, and Natasha sighed. Darya was exasperating, but she wasn't unkind. Not on purpose. Just, some of her bids for attention were better than others.

Natasha caught the tail of a memory, from when Natasha and Darya had been closer. Darya had developed an impressive array of silly voices, and as a second grader, she'd gone through a phase of talking out of the side of her mouth like a truck driver. Her deep belly laugh—coming from such a little girl—had made everyone near her laugh, too.

"Hey, I know," Darya said. Her tone was no longer glib. She was trying to fix things. "If you're allowed to go as someone fake, then dress up as a character from a Russian fairy tale." She slid into her seat and helped herself to some eggs. "Like that girl who was banished into the woods and torn to pieces by wild animals. You could be her."

Ava scrunched her forehead. "How am I supposed to dress up as a girl torn to pieces?"

"Okay, then go as the girl who was eaten by crows," Darya said. "What was her name?"

"*His* name was Prince Ivan, and he was a boy," Natasha said.

"Is it against the rules for a girl to dress up as a boy?" Darya said. She turned toward Ava. "If you don't want to be Prince Ivan, you could go as the boy sliced into pieces by his uncle. Or the kid who was thrown over a cliff. Or the girl who was forced to take a bath in boiling water and whose skin slipped off in long strips!"

"Darya, why would Ava want to dress up as a dead person?" Natasha said.

"Because it would be awesome! Because Russian fairy tales have the most awesome deaths ever!"

An illustrated collection of Russian fairy tales stood in the bookshelf in the den. It had belonged to Mama when she was younger, and the children in the fairy tales did come to extraordinarily gruesome ends.

If anyone ever wrote a fairy tale about Klara and the Three Little Girls, however, it would be the mother who met the terrible fate.

Well, *and* the daughters, since the daughters were the ones left behind.

But Mama, when she'd read the fairy tales to Natasha, had changed the stories any way she wanted. In Mama's versions, the children *didn't* die. The children escaped the crows and ran away from the cruel uncle. They only pretended to fall over the cliff.

Natasha recalled a story that Darya hadn't mentioned. It was about two maidens who lived in a castle, one with yellow hair and one with black. They were the best of friends and loved each other like sisters, but over time, the black-haired maiden grew jealous of the yellow-haired maiden's grace and beauty. One day she told the king a lie: that the yellow-haired maiden snuck out of the castle every night and danced until dawn with the *domovye*, the Russian version of elves.

The king was furious. He sliced off the yellow-haired maiden's head, and in the book version, the girl's head stayed sliced off. Too bad, so sad.

In Mama's version, the girl with black hair wept with remorse and scooped up her friend's head, cradling it in her arms. She kissed her friend's cheek, put the head back on the body, and tied it in place with a ribbon.

"Ava, blow your nose," Natasha said. "Darya, eat your breakfast." She scooted back her chair and strode toward the back door.

"What about my presentation?" Ava said. "Wh-where are you going?"

"To Papa's workshop. You can bring one of his lutes."

Natasha grabbed her coat from the closet, buttoning it up as she crunched across the new snow blanketing the yard. Flakes drifted lazily down.

She knocked on the door to Papa's workshop. She got no response, so she turned the knob and stepped inside.

"Papa?" she said.

He snored and shifted on the battered mattress in the corner of the room. He slept out here more often than he slept in the house.

"I'm borrowing one of your lutes," she said. "Ava needs it for a project."

Papa stirred in his sleep. Natasha sighed and went to him, pulling up the worn quilt so that it covered his shoulder.

She lifted one of the finished lutes from the rack by Papa's workbench. The one she picked was made of maple, swirled through with burls. Its soundboard was the shape of a teardrop, and in the middle of the teardrop, Papa had carved a lattice-covered hole, which on a lute was called a rose. When the strings of the lute were plucked, the rose amplified the resulting sound waves. That's how the music was made.

Natasha couldn't do it, though. Play the lute.

Neither could Ava. Neither could Darya.

Papa could, though it had been a long time since he had.

And Mama used to play the lute. Her slim fingers had danced over the strings, and she sang folk songs from Russia that made four-year-old Natasha dance, or try to, which made Mama and Papa laugh.

She carried the lute carefully, balancing it on her upraised knee as she closed the door of Papa's studio. It had stopped snowing, but she shielded the lute with her coat out of habit. Lutes were delicate instruments.

Halfway across the yard, she drew up short. There was a stone lying on the snow-packed path between Papa's studio and the house. No, two stones. The bottom stone was large and round and flattish, like a pancake. The second stone sat on top of the pancake stone. It was gray, about the size of a plump strawberry. Between the two stones was a creased piece of paper. The wind fluttered its edges, revealing a blur of words.

Goose bumps rose on Natasha's skin.

She stepped closer and knelt, taking care not to bump the lute. She pulled free the note, which was folded into fourths. On the uppermost side, in neat, precise handwriting, it said *Natasha*.

CHAPTER EIGHT

You don't know how special you are.
Lots of people don't know how special you are.
But I do.
And you are.

Natasha read it over and over. Five times, six times, seven. She traced the crease marks in the paper. She read the words again:

But I do. And you are.

She felt transported, like when she woke up in time to see the sun rise over a world that was still and quiet and perfect.

Someone thought she was special.

Her.

Natasha.

But . . . who?

She rose and glanced around, but there was no one in sight. There were footprints, but there were footprints everywhere. Ava had danced in the yard yesterday afternoon. Papa walked from the house to his studio three or four times daily. The aunts came outside too, for this reason or that.

Farther away were more footprints, a gray, slushy trail of them. Kids often cut across Natasha's yard to get to Laurel Street, where the junior high was.

Benton, for example. Benton cut through Natasha's yard on the way to school, and occasionally Natasha got lucky and was able to follow him all the way there. It was a hit-or-miss proposition, because on any given day Benton could be late to school, early to school, or just on time. She couldn't pin down his schedule because he didn't have a schedule, and she wasn't about to be a stalker girl, lurking behind Papa's studio until she saw Benton so that she could pop out and casually say, "Oh! Benton! Let's walk to school together, shall we?"

That would be creepy.

Natasha looked at the note again. The stones. The emptiness around her.

What if the person who left the note was creepy? What if he (or she) was a stalker?

Or . . . what if someone was playing a joke on her? She turned the idea over in her head. It was such a nice note. If it *was* a prank, it was terribly cruel.

She folded it and put it in her pocket. She hurried to the house with the lute.

"Here," she said, propping it against the wall inside the door.

"Thank you, Natasha," said Aunt Elena, who was back in the kitchen washing dishes. "Such a good idea."

"Papa said it was okay?" Ava said.

"Papa's fine with it." Natasha grabbed her backpack, slung it over her shoulder, and headed back to the door.

"Don't you want to wait for your sister?" Aunt Elena asked.

Natasha glanced at Darya. "She's too slow," she said.

"*She's* too fast," Darya said.

Aunt Elena shook her head. Natasha and Darya used to walk to school together, years ago. Then, at some point, they stopped. It wasn't due to some dreadful rift. They were just different.

Aunt Elena didn't ask if Natasha wanted to wait for Ava, because the sixth graders started later than the seventh and eighth graders.

"Your cheeks are *really* red," said Darya, scrutinizing Natasha.

Natasha touched her fingers to her face. "Yeah, well . . . it's cold outside," she said. "Okay. Bye!" She hurried out of the house.

As she walked, she thought about the note. By the time she reached the snow-cleared sidewalks of Laurel Street, she'd convinced herself that it *had* to be someone from school who'd left it for her. Someone who took the shortcut behind Papa's studio.

Someone like Benton, was the answer pushing hardest to be heard.

But it wasn't Benton. It couldn't have been. Why would Benton have left her a note?!

"You *did* wish to be someone's favorite," the Bird Lady said, appearing from behind a street sign.

Natasha screamed, then clamped her hand over her mouth. She looked at the signpost. It was made of steel, like any other signpost. It was slightly wider than her forearm, like any other signpost. *It was not big enough for someone to hide behind.* Not even a person as tiny as the Bird Lady.

Natasha straightened her spine. "Other people take that shortcut, too," she pointed out. "Dave Smith, Dave Winters, Marissa Owens. Any of them could have left the note."

"What note?" the Bird Lady said, blinking her round eyes.

Natasha dug her mittened fingers into her palms. It was none of the Bird Lady's business who left the note—and hold on. *Hold. On.* How did she know about Natasha's wish???

Natasha folded her arms over her chest. "Who *are* you?"

The Bird Lady's face softened. "Coo-ee," she said. "Sweet, silly girl."

"Did *you* write the note?" Natasha demanded.

"I most certainly didn't," the Bird Lady said with a giggle. She reached out as if to stroke Natasha's face, and Natasha stepped back. She tripped and went down hard, her backpack slipping free and spilling its contents onto the sidewalk.

"Ow," Natasha said.

"Cluck, cluck, cluck," the Bird Lady said. She squatted awkwardly and began shuffling Natasha's belongings back into her backpack.

Natasha's chest tightened. She wanted to tell the Bird Lady not to touch her stuff. She also wanted to tell her that people didn't say "cluck, cluck, cluck"; they just . . . clucked their tongues, if for whatever reason they felt compelled to do so. Like, if Natasha were writing a story, a sentence might be, "The old lady clucked when she saw the girl go sprawling on the sidewalk." A normal person would understand such a sentence perfectly. A normal person wouldn't assume the old lady actually said, "Cluck, cluck, cluck."

Natasha shut her eyes and drove the heels of her palms into her eye sockets. The real problem wasn't the clucking or the stuff-touching. It was the confusing mix of emotions the Bird Lady stirred up. Natasha found her annoying, yes, but undeniably fascinating. She was mysterious and weird and knew about things she shouldn't—like Natasha's wish.

The note.

Mama.

It would be best for everyone, Natasha concluded, if the Bird Lady just . . . disappeared, taking the secrets she shouldn't know with her.

"Go away, please," Natasha said.

Natasha heard the Bird Lady sigh. She heard the

pop of stiff joints and opened her eyes to see the Bird Lady struggling to her feet. She was sporting the same fuzzy pajama bottoms she'd worn before, and the same scarf trailed past her shoulders.

At least there's not a bird in her hair, Natasha thought.

Except—*oh.* The sparrow *was* there, fighting its way through the tangle of gray. Its beak emerged first, then its head, and finally its plump body and small wings. It shook itself and got resettled. It eyed Natasha with resentment.

Well, I don't like you either, Natasha thought.

Immediately, she felt ashamed. The bird was just a bird. Maybe Natasha *would* like it if she got to know it. She didn't know! She didn't know anything these days!

She scrambled up and jostled her backpack so that her books and notebooks slid in. She zipped the zipper tight.

"Have a good day, cupcake," the Bird Lady said. She held out a tight white rectangle. "And you don't want to forget this, now do you?"

The note! Natasha snatched it and hurried off. If, later, she discovered that the Bird Lady *had* written it, she'd rip it to shreds. But the Bird Lady claimed she hadn't. Plus, the Bird Lady was *old*. Too old and creaky to have placed a note in Natasha's yard and then dashed here, somehow managing to reach Laurel Street before Natasha showed up.

Natasha put several blocks between them before slowing down and allowing herself to check that the note was unharmed.

She unfolded it.

She sucked in her breath.

It wasn't the note she'd found outside Papa's workshop. It was new.

CHAPTER NINE

You don't know how beautiful you are, either.
You should smile more, Natasha. When you smile, it
lights up your face.

Natasha read it through twice. Then she dug in her
pocket for the first note. She shook it open, and her
eyes went from one to the other. She checked the handwriting, the funny little *a*s and the carefully dotted *i*s.
She went back and forth until she convinced herself of
the truth: There were *two* notes, both written to her,
both equally wondrous.

"Hi, Natasha," someone said, and she startled. It

was Benton's best friend, Stanley, looking round and puffy in a green down jacket that probably came from his parents' sporting goods store.

Natasha pressed the notes together and held them at her side, hidden by her cupped hand.

"Hi, Stanley," she said. Her legs felt hollow, and although she liked Stanley, she wasn't in the mood for a chat. She willed him to continue on toward wherever he was headed.

He didn't. He stood there, smiling awkwardly. They both smiled awkwardly, until the fog lifted from Natasha's brain.

Oh, right, she thought. *School.*

She started walking, and Stanley fell in beside her. Their strides were similar, which meant Natasha could neither pass him nor let him pass her without being obvious about it.

"I like your coat," he said.

"You do?" she said. Her coat was blue and plain and made of wool.

He nodded.

"Um, I like yours, too," she said.

Their boots clumped along the sidewalk. Natasha wanted to ask Stanley about Benton, but what would she say? *Hey, Stanley, does Benton like me? So* junior high, and even though Natasha was in junior high, she refused to be that undignified.

Plus, she would never be able to get the words out. Never ever ever.

She considered asking him about the Bird Lady, but ran into the same problem.

You know, the old lady who says "coo-ee" and "cluck, cluck, cluck"? she imagined herself saying. *The one with the bird in her hair?* It wasn't really a conversational winner, either.

They arrived at school and parted ways, and Natasha's shoulders finally relaxed.

When lunchtime came, Natasha saw Stanley again.

Natasha sat with Molly, as usual, and Stanley sat with Benton, as usual. Stanley wasn't wearing his puffy green coat anymore, and his basic blue T-shirt was too big on his thin frame. Benton, on the other hand, looked insanely adorable in his random-on-purpose T-shirt of the day. It was gray, with cartoon drawings of two old men on the front. The old men were wearing suits and ties, and their expressions were stern. Beneath them, in bold block letters, was the phrase HATERS GONNA HATE.

It looked soft, Benton's shirt. It wasn't too loose or too tight, and Natasha could tell he had muscles all over the place. Muscles for writing notes? Well. That was silly. But muscles for sprinting from one place to another, and then away again without ever being seen?

"Omigosh," Molly said. She snapped her fingers in front of Natasha's face. "Natasha. Na*ta*sha!"

"Huh?" Natasha said.

"You're staring at Benton," Molly said. "More than usual, even. Just go over to him and say, 'Hey, hot stuff, wanna go fishing?'"

"Fishing?" Natasha said.

"Or ice-skating! Or rock climbing!"

"Excellent ideas, but I don't think so. But terrific brainstorming." She gave Molly a thumbs-up.

Molly studied her for a long moment. "You're too happy," she said. "There's something going on, isn't there?"

"Of course not," Natasha said.

"Oh, right, of *course* not," Molly repeated. "Natasha, what aren't you telling me?"

"Nothing!"

"That's your answer? Really? 'Cause I know you, and you're hiding something. Why do you never tell me stuff?"

"I tell you tons of stuff!" Natasha protested. "Why don't *you* tell *me* stuff?"

Molly tilted her head. "Like how Zara hurt my feelings when she said I was too loud? Like how I want to whiten my teeth, but my mom won't let me, so I try to smile just using my lips?"

"You have a great smile," Natasha said, her heart beating a little too fast. "Your teeth are perfect."

"Like how it makes me sad when you keep everything to yourself?" Molly pressed.

Natasha held still, hit by a realization she didn't know what to do with. She *did* keep big chunks of her life from Molly. The notes, for example. Why hadn't she told Molly about the notes?

"Molly . . ." Natasha said.

Molly rubbed her forehead. Then she sighed and placed her palms on the table. She leaned in and said, "Do you have intimacy issues? Is that why you keep everything locked inside?"

Natasha stiffened, and she felt the sudden shock of tears.

Molly reddened. "Never mind. Forget I said that. *Intimacy issues.* What a stupid term anyway, right?" She hesitated. "But if you ever *do* want to tell me anything . . ."

Natasha felt exposed. What had begun as an ordinary conversation had crossed into unknown territory.

"Natasha?" Molly said. Her voice was small. "Are you mad at me? Did I make you mad?"

"No!" Natasha said.

"Then why are your eyes all wide?"

Natasha's heart pounded. She took a breath. "There *is* something I kind of want to tell you, but it's embarrassing."

"I won't be weird about it. I promise."

"You already know, anyway," Natasha said. "It's just . . . you're right. I do have a crush on Benton."

Molly squealed.

"Molly! *Shhhh!*"

"That was my happy noise!" Molly protested. "You have a crush on him, and you finally admitted it! I'm so proud of you!" She reached across the table and patted Natasha's head. "Has anything, you know, *happened* between you two?"

"Not really," Natasha said. Although earlier, in history class, she'd asked Benton what set of questions they were supposed to be working on, and he'd said, "Five through ten, and if you finish those, go on through fifteen."

"Oh," she'd said. "Thanks."

"No problem," he'd said, and his easy smile had made Natasha's cheeks grow warm.

"Then that's our next step," Molly announced. "To *make* something happen. *Ooo!* You should go over to him!"

"I don't think so."

"You could give him your apple!"

"Um, no."

"Why not? You could give him food, because guys like food, and he would fall in love with you. You guys would be *so cute* together! You'd be . . . Nabenton!"

"Nabenton?"

"Nataben? Nenton? Or, I know!" Molly clapped. "Bentasha! It's perfect!"

Natasha tilted her head, weighing the sound of it. *Bentasha*. It did sound good. She was about to say so when Molly got a funny expression on her face.

"What?" Natasha said. She looked where Molly was looking, and her heart sank.

Belinda Berry stood next to Benton, chatting and twirling her hair. She was a hair-twirling expert. Benton said something and patted the spot beside his lunch tray, and she laughed. Then she shrugged, turned sideways, and boosted herself onto the table. She perched on the edge and swung her legs.

"It doesn't necessarily *mean* anything," Molly said.

Benton grabbed Belinda's feet. She was wearing big

fuzzy boots, the kind Darya hated. Her legs were bare, and her skirt was short. She was cute and bubbly and *nice*—she really was—and Natasha couldn't compete with her in a million years. The magic it would take to make such a thing possible . . .

"Belinton," she said desolately.

"No," Molly moaned. "Bentasha is *so* much better."

A guy with even bigger muscles than Benton's sauntered toward Benton and Belinda. It was Dave Smith. He fist-bumped Benton and ruffled Belinda's hair, reaching up a bit to do so. Belinda smiled and caught his hand in hers. She slid off the table and nestled up beside him.

"Omigosh," Molly whispered. "Omigosh!"

Dave looped his arm over Belinda's shoulders. Belinda slipped her arm around Dave's waist. She rose up on her toes and let him kiss her, a sweet quick peck on the lips.

"Bedave," Molly said, turning to Natasha. A grin stretched across her face.

"Dalinda," Natasha said.

Molly held up her palm. Natasha gave her a high five.

I wish Klara wasn't so sad.
I wish I could make her feel better.
—ELENA KOVROV, AGE THIRTEEN

CHAPTER TEN

A week passed. Natasha didn't receive any more notes.

Another week passed, and on Friday, Natasha's English teacher talked to the class about "the ides of March." Natasha already knew what the ides of March were. It was a fancy way of saying March fifteenth, which was tomorrow, and which was Ava's birthday.

Tomorrow, Ava would turn twelve, which meant that she'd be the same age as Darya. She and Darya would both be twelve until Darya's birthday in August, when Darya would turn thirteen. Then Darya and Natasha would both be thirteen until Natasha's birthday rolled around again in November.

It wasn't a normal family configuration, Natasha knew. Papa and Mama had popped out three baby girls in quick succession, *bam bam bam*. But it was normal for Natasha. She was used to it. She knew nothing else, since Darya had come along before Natasha was a year old, and Ava had joined the pack less than a year after that.

"Ava came early" was her autopilot response when kids asked how the three sisters could be so close in age. Early and teensy and perfect, twelve years ago tomorrow.

As Natasha walked from English class to her locker, she thought about her birthday present for Ava. It was a gold necklace with a crystal-encrusted heart dangling from the middle. It glittered and sparkled, just right for Ava.

The hall was packed with kids. The air smelled like books and Pop-Tarts. Outside, the weather was gloomy, but inside, everything was bright and cozy. Everyone was cheerful, including Natasha.

She reached her locker, twisted the lock, and pulled on the latch. It didn't open. She banged it with her fist. It still didn't open. Benton saw her struggling with it, and he strode over and banged on it himself. The door sprang open.

"Thanks," Natasha said.

"No problem," Benton said. He turned to go.

"But I banged on it too," she said, casting about for a way to keep him there longer. "Why did it work for you and not for me?"

Benton turned back. "You have to hit it in the right spot."

"I did!"

"Well, and you kind of have to be me. I *am* pretty awesome."

"*Ohhhh*, of course," Natasha said, fizzy with delight. They were *flirting*, maybe-possibly-practically. She fought not to smile too widely. "What was I thinking?"

Benton grinned. Then he looked worried. "You do know I'm kidding, right?"

"Wait—you're *not* awesome?"

"No, I am, but . . ."

He floundered. Natasha kept her expression innocent, but on the inside, she was buzzing.

He crossed his arms over his chest, leaned back on his heels, and said, "Ah-*ha*. Pretty tricky, Natasha Blok."

The way he spaced out the syllables was adorable: *prih-tee trih-kee.*

The way he said her name made her skin tingle.

"That was funny," Benton said, nodding. "That was good." He looked at her in a new way. "There's more to you than people think, isn't there?"

"Benton!" a guy called from down the hall. "Dude, you're holding us up!"

"Dude, chill," Benton called back. Then he said, "All right, well, see you around, Natasha," and he loped off to join his friends.

That afternoon, Natasha lay on her bed and re-played the moment. She tried to decide what it meant, if it had meant anything at all.

She wanted it to have meant something, very much. But could *wanting* something make it come true? Because on her Wishing Day, Natasha's last wish had been to be someone's favorite. To be seen as special just for being herself.

Benton's notes (which was how she thought of them, even though she didn't know for sure that he'd written them) had made her feel special. Absolutely! And today, when he looked at her the way he did, that made her feel special too. When he'd said there was more to her than people thought, her stomach had flipped over.

Except then he took off without a backward glance. He said, "See you around," but there wasn't anything special about "see you around."

So it was confusing. He'd flirted with her at her locker, but he never beckoned her over during lunch, like he had with Belinda. He never patted the table he was sitting at, encouraging her to hop up on it so they could talk.

And! Who said the notes were from Benton anyway?! She'd let herself imagine that he'd written them, and somehow the possibility of Benton being her secret admirer had lodged in her heart as truth. But what if that was just wishful thinking?

Wishful thinking. Of course it was wishful thinking. Making wishes, by definition, was wishful thinking.

Natasha sighed. She had a hard time imagining herself *ever* perching on a lunchroom table, to be honest. But maybe thinking wishfully required taking risks. Maybe she *could* be that girl, adored by a boy who grabbed her feet and playfully swung them back and forth.

Or not.

She stared at the ceiling, which was a good ceiling, with a familiar pattern of cracks that she'd turned into a multitude of things over the years. An old man's profile. A chapel. A duck.

Today she made a question mark out of the cracks. It was a stretch, but it suited her purpose. There were so many things she didn't know!

Her third Wishing Day wish was to be somebody's favorite. The wish before that was to be kissed, and according to the Wishing Day rules, she was supposed to make that wish come true herself.

But how???

Benton was the boy she wanted to be kissed by, if she was going to be kissed by anyone. But what was she supposed to do? Approach him in the hall, grab his shoulders, and pucker up? Find him in the cafeteria and say, "Hey, Benton, want to smooch?" Hide by the path he took to school and pounce on him when he came strolling along?

No, no, and no, with an especially big no to the hide-by-the-path scenario. She'd scare him to death if she sprang out at him with no warning. She'd scare herself to death. They'd both fall over, dead, and foxes would feast on their bodies.

Or, worse, she'd jump out, waggle her hands and arms, and go "Boogidy-boogidy-boo!" like the bogey-man. She wouldn't *want* to. She just would, accidentally, for the simple reason that the idea had floated into her imagination and was now lodged there forever.

Ugh. No. *You will* not *go* boogidy-boogidy-boo *to Benton, Natasha*, she told herself firmly. *Understand?*

She shifted positions, taking her hands out from beneath her head and splaying her arms wide, palms up. She tried to relax her muscles and let them "fall off her bones," a phrase she'd picked up from her gym teacher during a unit on yoga.

It was a horrible phrase when taken literally. Wonderfully horrible, and she and Molly had latched onto it for that very reason. For almost a month, they let their muscles fall off their bones every chance they got.

"Sorry, Mom, but I can't," Molly would call from her bedroom, when her mother asked her to come back downstairs and clean up her dishes. "I'm letting my muscles fall off my bones!"

Or Molly and Natasha would flop onto the lawn of the school courtyard and spread out their arms and legs like stars.

"What's new?" Natasha would ask.

"Oh, nothing, just letting my muscles fall off my bones," Molly would say. "You?"

"Same."

Natasha smiled, remembering. She *could* call Molly now, if she wanted. She could say, "Hey, dollface. Are your bones falling off your body?" Wait. Not bones, muscles. "Are your *muscles* falling off your bones?"

Then she could ask Molly for her advice. She could kill two birds with one stone. (Another dreadful expression, if you thought about it. Why kill the birds at all?) But she could ask Molly how to proceed with Benton, and that would prove to Molly that she didn't have intimacy issues. That she *did* open up to her.

She owed Molly a call, regardless. Molly was going out of town next week for a family thing, which meant she would miss the Spring Festival. But Molly was okay with it because her parents were taking her to some big outlet mall to shop for a dress, because the family thing was something she had to be fancy for.

Her cousin's bar mitzvah. That's what it was. Molly had been talking about it all week, and today at lunch, she'd said, "Omigosh, and I haven't even described my aunt and uncle's house to you. What is wrong with me?"

Then the bell had rung, and Molly had groaned. "Remind me to tell you about my aunt and uncle's house. It's seriously a mansion. Okay?"

Hmm, Natasha thought, shifting again on her bed. She was fine with hearing about Molly's aunt and uncle's house, but maybe not right now.

She could get out her journal, she supposed. Writing things down might make them clearer.

Or she could do push-ups, which her gym teacher said were an excellent all-body workout.

She sighed and shifted positions, stretching her legs out long and pointing her toes. She pulled her pillow into a better position beneath her head and continued to stare at the ceiling.

CHAPTER ELEVEN

Saturday night was game night at the Blok house. Aunt Elena was the one who'd started the tradition, and she was the one who came up with the games. Aunt Elena told Natasha and Darya it was for Ava, because Ava was the youngest, and Ava liked playing games. But Natasha knew that Aunt Elena liked playing games, too.

In the past, they'd played Rat-a-Tat Cat or Trouble or Monopoly, but Monopoly had been taken out of rotation because it took so long, and because Darya got overly competitive when it came to getting Boardwalk and Park Place.

Aunt Elena came up with nongame games, too. Games that were actually activities devised to make everyone laugh. Last month, Aunt Elena instructed everyone to stick their elbows out in front of them (one elbow per person) while lifting their hands to their shoulders (one hand per person, the hand that "belonged" with the lifted elbow).

Then Aunt Elena went around and balanced a quarter on each person's upraised elbow. The goal, she said, was for everyone to cup their hands and then whip them down, fast enough to catch the falling quarter.

Aunt Vera's quarter kept plonking to the floor. "My elbows are too pointy!" she'd complained.

Darya had mastered the trick quickly. She'd place a quarter on her elbow, swish her hand down in a graceful arc, then flip her hand over and open it. "Did it!" she'd cry, revealing the captured quarter.

Ava, Aunt Elena, and Natasha were good at it as well. Along with Darya, they'd started adding quarters to make the challenge harder. Two quarters. Three quarters. Four quarters balanced neatly on top of their elbows, then caught just as neatly when they whipped down their hands. Or clattering noisily to the floor. It went both ways.

Papa would have been good at it, Natasha suspected,

because he was good with his hands. But although he'd stuck around and watched for ten or so minutes, he hadn't participated.

"Just once, Papa," Ava had pleaded. "Just try once. Come on."

"I'm too old for games," he'd said. Then he'd smiled vaguely, ruffled Ava's hair, and headed back to his workshop.

Aunt Elena had been the grand winner that night, ultimately balancing twenty quarters on her elbow and catching every single one.

"Impressive," Natasha had said.

"Why thank you," Aunt Elena had replied, her cheeks flushed and her hair coming loose from her ponytail.

Tonight, for Ava's birthday, Aunt Elena came up with a game that would appeal especially to her. They'd already had Ava's favorite meal for dinner, spaghetti with meatballs. They'd sung to Ava and eaten cake and passed out presents, and Ava had beamed.

"Next year, I'll be thirteen," she'd said.

"But not until after *I* turn thirteen," Darya had said. "I'll turn thirteen before you do."

"Duh," Ava had said.

"But as of tonight, you are twelve, and that's cool,

too," Natasha had said. "Sheesh, Darya. Can you let Ava have this one night all to herself?"

Now, with the dinner dishes put away, Aunt Elena called everyone around the kitchen table and told them to take a seat.

"Peppermint Patties," Ava said, eyeing a large ceramic bowl full of shiny, foil-wrapped mints. "Yummy. Are they Birthday Peppermint Patties?"

"Where's Nate?" Aunt Elena said, scanning the room. She opened the back door and sighed when she saw the lights on in Papa's workshop. "Nate?" she called. "Na-ate!"

"Let's just play," Darya said.

"How *do* we play?" Ava asked.

"Yes, Elena," Aunt Vera said. She strode to Aunt Elena, reached past her, and closed the door. "Illuminate us."

Aunt Elena turned toward the table. Natasha caught a glimpse of sadness before she shook it off, smiled, and took her seat.

"The goal is *not* to eat them," Aunt Elena said, batting Ava's hand from the bowl.

Ava made a sound of protest. She was wearing her new necklace, the one with the heart on it that Natasha had given her. It looked pretty.

"Not right away," Aunt Elena said. She selected a Peppermint Pattie and unwrapped it. It was nearly the same size as a quarter. "The goal"—she tilted her face to the ceiling and put the Peppermint Pattie on her forehead—"is to get it into your mouth without using your hands. *Then* you can eat it."

As she talked, the movement of her jaw made the mint slip off her forehead. It landed on the table, and she laughed. She tried again, and by doing a lot of undignified tensing and wiggling of her facial muscles, she was able to navigate the mint all the way down to the bridge of her nose, at which point it once again fell off.

Everyone laughed.

The chocolate coating was beginning to melt, and when Aunt Elena put the mint on her forehead for a third time, her fingers came away sticky. She contorted her face to move the mint, and this time, as it inch-wormed down her face, it left a trail of chocolate. But by tilting her head sideways, she got the mint onto her cheek, and from there, precariously into her mouth.

"Yes!" she said, thrusting her fist into the air. She chewed and swallowed and grinned. "Score!"

"I want to try," Ava said, grabbing a mint.

Natasha and Darya each took one too. So did Aunt

Vera, though she simply unwrapped hers and popped it into her mouth.

"Hey! Cheating!" Ava cried.

"Vera, that was *very* naughty," Aunt Elena scolded. "Do you understand, or do I need to give you a time-out?"

Aunt Vera rolled her eyes. "You have chocolate on your cheek."

Natasha giggled. Her aunts were fun when they were in moods like this. Next to her, Ava scrunched and unscrunched her nose intently. She tried to watch the Peppermint Pattie's progress, which made her cross-eyed.

Natasha glanced at Darya, and they shared a smile. They looked away quickly—both of them—but Natasha felt happy.

After several tries, Ava got her mint into her mouth. She high-fived everyone and said, "Yes!" just like Aunt Elena had. And, like Aunt Elena, she had chocolate smeared all over her.

She grabbed a second mint, unwrapped it, and said, "Silas would *not* be good at this." She paused and tilted her head. "Or maybe he would. Would he?"

"Who's Silas?" Natasha asked.

"A boy in my class. He goes to Ms. J for tutoring

too, but he doesn't like her to say it out loud."

"Say what out loud?" Darya said.

"'Silas, isn't it time for you to go to tutoring?'" she said in a voice that was an awful lot like Aunt Vera's. She switched back to her normal voice. "He doesn't like people to know. I told him it doesn't matter, but . . ."

She shrugged and licked a smudge of chocolate from her finger. "Anyway, he has such a tight grip that I can't unfurl his fingers *at all*, not once he's latched onto me."

For a moment, no one responded.

Then Natasha said, "Why does he *grip* you?"

"Because he likes me. And by the way, there is one thing about being me that I *don't* like, and it's that Silas always wants to play with me during recess, and so does Melody and so does Alvinia. So do a lot of people. But Alvinia wants me all to herself, and I don't know what to do because I don't want to hurt anyone's feelings."

"Oh," Natasha said. She frowned. When she was in the sixth grade, did she have playground problems? No, because she read books, usually. She got permission to spend recess in the library. Or, on the days she didn't, she strolled with Molly around the playground's perimeter, listening and laughing as Molly babbled about whatever.

"Can't you play with all of them?" she said. "Or, like, rotate?"

"Did you not hear a word she said?" Darya asked. "*No*. She can't."

"Darya, watch your tone," Aunt Elena warned.

Ava looked at Natasha kindly. She patted her hand and said, "It's okay. Mainly I was just saying that everyone thinks it's so great to be popular, but sometimes it wears me out."

"*Yeah*, Natasha," Darya said. She turned to Ava. "I understand, because I'm popular, too. Natasha just doesn't know what it's like."

"*Darya,*" Aunt Elena and Aunt Vera said at the same time.

Natasha wasn't as bothered by Darya's comment as her aunts seemed to be. It stung, and Darya was being a jerk, but in Darya's mind, she probably thought she was being funny.

And Natasha *wasn't* popular. So? Everyone was different, including Ava and Darya. They were both popular, but not in the same way. Darya wouldn't choose Ava's friends, Natasha suspected, and vice versa.

"Also?" Ava said. Her mint fell off her face and she groaned. She leaned down and picked it up. "Alvinia

115

just makes me mad sometimes, because yesterday I told her I *would* play with her, but that we had to let Melody play too or that would be mean, and I definitely didn't want to be mean with my birthday right around the corner. And Alvinia started *crying*, only it was fake crying. And then she ran to Ms. Gupta and said she'd been bitten by a butterfly! And Ms. Gupta let her go to the office and get a cold pack!"

"Wow," Darya said. She caught her mint when it fell off her brow and just ate it.

"What?" Natasha said. "Butterflies don't *bite*."

"I know! There weren't even any butterflies around! She basically got a cold pack for nothing, and now she's going around telling everyone how scary butterflies are!"

"Butterflies aren't scary," Natasha said. She felt outraged that this Alvinia person had suggested otherwise.

"Of course butterflies aren't scary," Aunt Elena said. "My grandmother, who was you girls' great-grandmother, said that butterflies represent rebirth."

"And rebirth *isn't* scary?" Darya said. "Um, zombies, anyone?"

"Our grandmother also said never to leave an empty bottle on the counter," Aunt Vera replied archly.

"Otherwise it will soon be filled with tears."

Everyone gave that some thought.

"How do the tears get in the bottle?" Ava asked.

"You'd have to cry right into it," Darya said. "Or use the bottle as a Kleenex."

"*No,*" Ava said.

"Or put Alvinia in a room with lots of butterflies, and put the bottle in there too," Darya went on. "It could be a test. If Alvinia *was* scared of butterflies, she'd cry, right? If she filled the bottle with tears, she could prove it."

"There *aren't* any butterflies in the winter!" Ava said. "Which is how I *know* Alvinia didn't get bitten by one, because it's too cold!" She huffed. "What I *don't* know is what the butterflies do when it's this cold. Where do they go?"

"France," Darya said.

"Some fly to warmer places," Aunt Elena said. "Others hibernate."

"Butterflies *hibernate*?" Ava said.

"They tuck themselves into the snuggest spots they can find," Aunt Elena said. "Beneath the loose bark on trees, or inside a rotten log. They stay there until spring comes, and then they wake up."

Aunt Elena glanced at Aunt Vera. "It truly is

magical, if you think about it."

"If you say so," Aunt Vera said.

"I do," Aunt Elena replied.

"Did Mama?" Ava piped up.

"What do you mean, Ava?" Aunt Elena asked. "Did Klara what?"

Ava grew uncomfortable. "Just, was she on your side or Aunt Vera's? About the butterflies. Did she . . . you know . . ."

She didn't complete her sentence, but she didn't need to, not for Natasha.

Did Mama believe that butterflies were magic? That's what Ava wanted to know.

"Never mind," Ava said.

Natasha sensed the barest flicker of a memory. She strained to catch it, but it had already fluttered away.

CHAPTER TWELVE

There was a Johnny Cash song Natasha liked. Papa used to sing it, accompanying himself on the lute. It was slow and melancholy, but exactly the *right* kind of melancholy—though Natasha suspected that such a sentiment wouldn't make sense to most people.

"'Cause there's something in a Sunday that makes a body feel alone." She loved that line. She understood that line. She, too, had felt alone when she woke up this morning. Everything was quiet. Everything was still. Outside, the snowy haze was infinite. Smoke curled from the chimneys of nearby houses, and that was the only indication that other people were out there, living their own Sunday mornings.

Natasha looked out her window for a long time. At some point, Ava started rustling about, and Natasha moved to the wall that separated their rooms. She could hear Ava humming. Sometimes Ava added words. The words had to do with Ava's hairbrush, from what Natasha could make out.

There was something reassuring about Ava's song. She was twelve now, but she was still Ava.

Natasha opened her door quietly and stepped into the hall. She padded past Ava's room, then past Darya's. Darya was dead asleep. Natasha had no doubt about that. She was nearly impossible to rouse on weekdays, and on weekends, she stayed in bed till noon if the aunts let her.

Her aunts' rooms were at the end of the hall. Aunt Elena had moved into the guest room, and Aunt Vera had taken over Mama and Papa's room. Not in a bad way; it was just that Papa never went in it anymore. He slept in his workshop, or downstairs on the sofa.

Natasha saw that Aunt Vera's door was open. Her bed was neatly made, and Natasha smelled the citrus scent of her shampoo, which meant she'd already showered. Soon, the smell of biscuits and bacon would fill the house. Aunt Vera believed in a hearty breakfast.

Aunt Elena's door was cracked, and the light was on, so Natasha knocked.

"Yes? Come in!" Aunt Elena called.

Aunt Elena's bed was a mess. Aunt Elena herself was in her bathroom, curling her hair. "Oh, Natasha," she said, turning a bit pink. "You must think I'm so silly, don't you?"

"Why?" Natasha said.

"Playing with hairstyles. You know." Her eyes brightened. "Want me to do yours?"

"No thanks," Natasha said, and Aunt Elena laughed.

"Maybe one day," she said.

"I doubt it," Natasha said.

"Well, sit and chat with me," Aunt Elena said, turning back to the mirror.

Natasha sat on the edge of the bathtub. She watched Aunt Elena clamp a strand of her brown hair in the curling rod and roll it up. Aunt Elena counted to ten—Natasha could see her lips moving—then slid the curling rod free. A shiny spiral curl bounced against her collarbone.

"I'll brush it out, don't worry," Aunt Elena said.

"In the end, it'll just be waves."

"Okay," Natasha said, though she hadn't been worried. "It looks pretty."

Aunt Elena smiled at Natasha in the mirror. "You think? Really?"

Natasha nodded. Aunt Elena was pretty no matter what. Her hair was several shades lighter than Natasha's, and she shared the same delicate features as Ava and Darya. Ava and Darya both took after Mama's side of the family (which was also Aunt Elena's side of the family), while Natasha, with her serious eyes and darker coloring, looked more like Papa.

"Can I ask you a question?" Natasha said.

"Sure," Aunt Elena said.

"It has to do with the Bird Lady."

In the mirror, she saw Aunt Elena's eyebrows lift.

"Ava made me think about it," Natasha went on. She found that she was clenching her fingers, and she made herself stop. "Because of how cold it is? And the butterflies? And just, you know . . ." She swept her hand to indicate Aunt Elena's bedroom window, its view similar to Natasha's. "Everyone stays in when the weather's like this, for the most part."

Aunt Elena curled another strand of hair.

"It's just . . . where does the Bird Lady go? Where

does she live? Where does she get her food?" Natasha's fingers folded into her palms again. "What's her deal?!"

"Natasha, I don't have an answer for you," Aunt Elena said. "I've wondered the same things myself, many times."

"Well, *that's* no help," Natasha said. She clapped her hand over her mouth. "Sorry."

"It's okay. You're right, it's not any help."

"She's so odd," Natasha said.

Aunt Elena nodded.

"She wears pajama pants. She lets a bird live in her hair!"

Aunt Elena lifted her shoulders. "Most people think she's bonkers."

"Do you?"

Aunt Elena studied her reflection. She shook out her hair to find any leftover straight parts, and when she did, she sectioned them out and curled them one by one.

"When I was nine, I climbed to the top of Willow Hill," she said. She bit her lip. "This story doesn't have to do with whether the Bird Lady is bonkers or not, actually. Or maybe it does. Huh, I don't know."

"Tell it," Natasha said.

"Well." Aunt Elena put down the curling rod and

unplugged it. She turned to Natasha. Her hair was a cascade of curls.

"I was nine, and at the top of Willow Hill, I saw the Bird Lady," she said. "She was threading her way in and out of the branches of the willow tree. You know the one."

The great willow. Natasha nodded.

"In and out, in and out, like a needle through cloth. It looked like she was scattering seeds, and . . ."

"And what?"

"I asked if I could help," Aunt Elena said sheepishly.

"Oh," Natasha said. She was touched by the image of Aunt Elena as a little girl, shyly approaching the Bird Lady.

"I asked if I could help, and the Bird Lady said, 'Took you long enough, didn't it?'" Aunt Elena lifted her eyebrows.

"Then she gave me a small leather pouch. Only instead of seeds, the pouch was filled with marshmallows."

"Marshmallows!"

"It's true. Vera never believed me, but your mother did."

Natasha swallowed. If Aunt Elena had been nine,

her mother, Klara, would have been ten. Two years younger than Ava was now.

"I started to scatter them as if they *were* seeds, but the Bird Lady put her hand on mine. 'You eat,' she told me. 'Not for the birds. For you.'"

"Was her hand wrinkly?" Natasha asked, remembering the day the Bird Lady gave her the second note. Her knuckles had been red, and her fingers had been stick-like and curved. Her skin had been as thin as crepe paper.

"I think her hand has always been wrinkly," Aunt Elena said.

"It couldn't have *always* been wrinkly. At one point, she must have been a girl herself."

Aunt Elena pursed her lips. "Can you imagine her as a girl?"

Natasha tried, but in her mind's eye, the Bird Lady refused to grow young. No backward time-lapse photography for her, no transformation from crone to matron to maid.

Crone, matron, maid. Where had those words come from? They were just fancy words for an old lady, a woman, and a girl, but it was disconcerting how they'd slipped into her thoughts from nowhere.

She gave herself a shake.

125

"I can't imagine the Bird Lady as a girl, no," Natasha said. She cleared her throat. Her voice sounded rusty. "Did you eat the marshmallows?"

"I did," Aunt Elena said. Her eyes twinkled. "I know, I know, never take candy from a stranger. But the Bird Lady wasn't a stranger, exactly . . ."

"She's just strange," Natasha finished.

"They were lighter than spun sugar," Aunt Elena said. "They were *extraordinary*, Natasha. They melted in my mouth, and *I* felt lighter than spun sugar. So light I could fly! I couldn't—yes, I tried—but for a week, my life was charmed. I was picked to feed our class hamster. My shoelaces never came untied, and my hair never got tangled. I found pennies on the sidewalk, and a blue glass egg. And for that entire week, no one got mad at me for anything, even Vera."

Aunt Elena stepped closer. She tucked Natasha's hair behind her ear. "And your mother and I? We built the *best* house of cards in the *history* of card houses."

Natasha smiled uncertainly. She had so many questions about Mama, but when Mama's name came up, she invariably got anxious.

Aunt Elena perched on the rim of the tub next to Natasha. "Your mother was always good at card houses. We'd have contests, Klara and I, and mine always fell down before hers."

She clasped Natasha's hands. "She took it very seriously. She built her houses to last."

A heaviness settled over Natasha. *Until it mattered*, she thought.

"What's that?"

Natasha blinked. Had she spoken the words aloud? "Nothing. Never mind. I have no idea."

Aunt Elena searched Natasha's expression, and Natasha brought back her stiff smile.

I'm smiling, see? she thought, although she kept her lips pressed together to make sure no words spilled out this time. *La la la, happy me. Go on and finish your story—doesn't that sound nice?*

"Natasha. Sweetheart."

"Tell me the rest," Natasha said brightly. *And don't call me sweetheart*, she pleaded silently. *Later, maybe, but not right now, because there's a lump already in my throat.*

Aunt Elena grew tender, which made Natasha want to run away.

"Anyway," she said. "Klara and I built a house of cards that was twenty-two stories high."

"Even more than the twenty quarters you balanced on your elbow," Natasha said.

Aunt Elena laughed. "Balanced and *caught*, thank you very much."

They sat quietly, but the might-accidentally-cry danger had passed. Natasha gently pulled her hand from Aunt Elena's and placed both of her palms flat on her thighs.

She thought about Aunt Elena and the Bird Lady. She thought about Mama and the Bird Lady.

I quite liked your mother, you know, the Bird Lady had said. Implying what? That the Bird Lady had known Mama? If so, how? In a marshmallow sort of way, or something deeper?

Though she was a silly girl, too, the Bird Lady had also said.

What had Mama done that was silly?

Natasha didn't want to ask Aunt Elena those questions, not now. Maybe she'd ask the Bird Lady herself, when and if she ran into her again. Wait, strike that. She'd ask her when and if she *encountered* her again. No more head-on collisions, please.

Natasha did have one last question for her aunt. She turned to look at her. "Aunt Elena?"

"Hmm?"

"Last night, when we were talking about butter-flies . . ."

Aunt Elena waited. Her gaze was steady and kind.

"*Did* Mama believe?"

"That they were magic?"

Natasha nodded.

"She did," Aunt Elena said with simple authority. "Klara believed there was magic in everything."

CHAPTER THIRTEEN

That afternoon, Natasha took a walk along the edge of City Park's frozen lake. The wind off the ice cut through her hat and scarf and coat and mittens, but it was worth it, because at home she'd been going stir crazy. She needed to move.

Two days earlier, on Friday, Benton had banged on her locker and made it open. That was the day she'd lain on her bed and thought about her third Wishing Day wish—to be someone's favorite—as well as her second Wishing Day wish—to be kissed.

She'd steered clear of her first Wishing Day wish, which was that Mama would come back.

Which was impossible.

But what if it wasn't? What if Natasha, like Mama, believed that there was magic in everything? If magic really existed, wouldn't *anything* be possible?

When Aunt Elena was nine, the Bird Lady had given her magical marshmallows, and she and Mama had built a twenty-two-story house out of playing cards.

Four years later, Aunt Elena had celebrated her Wishing Day. She'd never told anyone what she wished for (and Natasha had tried hard to persuade her, as had Darya and Ava), but she vowed that her wishes had come true.

Aunt Vera had been thirteen once, too. She'd had a Wishing Day just like every other girl in Willow Hill, although like Aunt Elena, she refused to say what she'd wished for. As a grown-up, Aunt Vera dismissed the Wishing Day tradition altogether. Actively. Vocally. Angrily.

But long ago, Natasha had overheard something not meant for her ears. It was after Mama had disappeared. The aunts were picking tomatoes, and Natasha was supposed to be helping, but she'd fallen asleep in the warm sun. She'd awoken groggily to hear Aunt Vera say, "Well, that was just coincidence."

"I don't believe that for an instant," Aunt Elena

had said. "The day after your Wishing Day, the very next day, your complexion just happened to clear up? Not a single bump or pimple left?"

At the moment, Natasha had just listened. Later, she'd thought it through more properly. Aunt Vera had wished for clear skin? What a trivial thing to use a wish on! Then Natasha had gone to the old photo albums, where she'd found a picture of Aunt Vera as a young girl. Her face had been red and scaly and covered with pockmarks, and Natasha had felt ashamed.

But that day in the garden, Aunt Elena had barreled on to a new topic. "And what about Roy?" she'd said. "Are you going to claim Roy was a coincidence too?"

"Roy?" Natasha had said aloud.

Aunt Vera had gasped, and Aunt Elena had pulled Natasha out from behind her sleeping tree, scolding her for spying.

"But I wasn't!" Natasha had protested. "Aunt Vera, who's Roy?"

Aunt Vera had blushed furiously. "We were young," she'd said in a strained voice. "It was a young romance. Now, *enough* is *enough*."

Out by City Park Lake, Natasha ducked her head against the cold. She sifted through memories, but her knowledge of Wishing Day magic was sparse.

Tessa Clarke, who was two years older than Natasha, supposedly wished that her mom would find her lost wedding ring. Tessa's mom supposedly did.

A girl named Ruby, who no longer lived in Willow Hill, had used one of her wishes to land a job in a big city. She was now a journalist in New York.

To make your Wishing Day magic stronger, some people said, you should find a purple pebble and clutch it in your right hand when you make your wishes.

Or, you should find a purple pebble and clutch it in your *left* hand while making your wishes.

Or, you should find a purple pebble and swallow it, wishing with all your might that you don't choke to death.

At some point, the lore surrounding Wishing Day magic always turned ridiculous.

Papa once talked to Natasha about Wishing Day. It was one of the few times after Mama disappeared when Natasha felt as if Papa was truly *there*, and not off in his head somewhere.

The two of them had been pulling weeds out by Papa's workshop. Natasha had been eight. She knew she'd been eight because when she was eight, she was in the second grade, and when she was in second grade, her class had studied Greek gods and goddesses.

"Ms. Florian said that the head honcho god was Zeus, and that he turned someone into a *goat*," Natasha had said. "I would *hate* to be turned into a goat!"

Papa had chuckled and assured her that there was little chance of that happening.

He'd been more present back then. He'd still had hope that Mama would magically reappear.

"I could *wish* to turn into a goat on my Wishing Day," Natasha had mused, "but I won't."

"Good," Papa had said.

"Or I could turn Darya into a goat! Or Aunt Vera!"

"Do you think a goat could make pancakes as well as Aunt Vera? And the laundry—she'd eat it instead of folding it."

Natasha had laughed. Then, sensing a rare opportunity, she'd pelted him with questions.

"Do Wishing Day wishes really work?"

"Depends on who you ask."

"Was it really someone in our family who brought the Wishing Day magic to Willow Hill? Do *you* believe in magic?"

"Hmm," Papa had said. "I suppose I do—but don't go telling your aunt Vera."

"I won't."

"But I don't know if the magic began with one specific person. I do know that your mother's side of the family seems to have a greater talent for magic than most."

"Really?"

Papa had studied her. "Your mother teemed with magic, Natasha. At times she was absolutely incandescent."

Natasha hadn't known what *teemed* meant, or *incandescent*. But she'd hurried to a new question, because Papa's eyes had grown misty. If he got too sad, he'd stop talking.

"Why don't boys have magic?" she'd asked. "Why don't boys have Wishing Days?"

Papa had taken a long time to answer, so long that Natasha had worried he wasn't going to. But after several minutes, he'd said, "Willow Hill was founded in 1766. Generations of children have grown up here."

Natasha had nodded.

"From what I've heard, boys did celebrate their Wishing Days once upon a time."

"Why 'once upon a time'?"

Papa had looked at Natasha straight on. "Your great-grandmother had a cousin who nearly lost his hand in a sawmill."

"Oh," she'd said, not understanding.

"He lost two fingers. His wrist got torn up, too. Came close to bleeding out, but the doctor cauterized his wounds and saved his life."

Natasha had stored *cauterized* away in her brain with the other new words.

"Funny thing, though," Papa had continued. "He had just turned thirteen, so his Wishing Day wasn't far off. And *after* his Wishing Day, his hand healed up, far more quickly than the doctor expected."

"But Papa," Natasha had said, disappointed. A hand mangled in a sawmill—that was exciting. The wounds healing? That was ordinary.

"His fingers grew back," Papa had said quietly.

Natasha had sucked in her breath. "Oh."

"That's the only story about a boy and magic that I've ever heard—and remember, he wasn't a regular town kid."

"Because he was in our family."

"The wishes most boys made *didn't* come true," Papa had said. "But it was different for the girls, even the girls not connected to your bloodline."

My bloodline, Natasha had repeated silently. The words made her brain feel stretchy, like taffy.

He'd shrugged. "My guess? After a while, the boys

gave up. After a longer while, the boys forgot that they'd given up. They forgot that the tradition ever involved them at all."

"The boys in my class make fun of Wishing Day," Natasha had said.

"Well, they would, wouldn't they?" Papa had replied, and that was the last he said about it.

Natasha continued along the path by the lake. Her nose was now at that yucky-runny-drippy stage where she couldn't help but use the back of her mitten to wipe it.

She thought about Mama, and how much Papa missed her. What if Mama fell and hit her head on the day she disappeared? What if she got amnesia, and whoever helped her took her to a hospital outside of Willow Hill? If Mama couldn't remember her name, then the hospital wouldn't have known who to notify.

Maybe, over time, Mama got better from the head wound, but the amnesia stuck.

And then, slowly-slowly, her memories started coming back. Her old life hovered just out of reach, and then—*swoosh*—it fell into place all at once, like Peter Pan regaining his shadow.

"It was just a misunderstanding," she'd say when she showed up at their door. "Natasha, you've grown so big! Darya, your hair is absolutely lovely—when did you learn to do updos? And Ava, little Ava . . . oh honey, I've *missed* you. I've missed all of you!"

Everyone would cry. Everyone would embrace. Aunt Vera and Aunt Elena would welcome back their sister with open arms. And then . . .

Papa would come in from his workshop, weary from the day's work.

Everyone would grow still. Then, as if they'd been cued, the aunts and the kids would part, letting Mama step forward into the light. Ava would keep holding her hand, maybe.

Papa would choke out a sob and say, "Klara!" He'd rush to her and hug her, hard hard hard. Everyone would cry some more, but it would turn to laughing-crying. Happy crying. Papa wouldn't leave Mama's side. He wouldn't stop gazing at her, not for a second, and his eyes would shine with love.

But that's not going to happen, Natasha reminded herself, embarrassed by the lump in her throat.

She picked her steps carefully. Sometimes her boot broke through a thin crust of ice on top of the snow, and she slipped, but she didn't fall.

It's not going to happen, she told herself, even more firmly. She tried to push down her bubble of hope.

When that didn't work, she tried a different tactic.

What if Mama came back—she wouldn't—but just say she did, and her return *wasn't* with hugs and laughter and happy tears?

Natasha had read a horrible story in English about a dried-up monkey's paw that granted three wishes to whoever owned it. A man grabbed it out of the fire after its previous owner tossed it in, and he wished for two hundred British pounds.

A few hours later, the man and his wife found out that their son had been killed at the factory where he worked. He'd fallen into a machine that ground things up (which wasn't so different from the sawmill Papa had told her about, come to think of it). At any rate, the man and his wife were given a lump sum of money as compensation—two hundred British pounds.

The man and the woman buried their son and tried to carry on. But the wife couldn't, and a week later, she grasped the monkey's paw and wished with all her heart that her boy was alive again. Soon afterward, the couple heard noises outside. Crawling, scrabbling, shuffling noises. Wet, ragged breaths. The wife didn't care, and when she heard a dull rap on the door, she ran to unbolt it.

The man, though. He knew. He'd seen his son's

body before he'd been buried. He also knew what happened to bodies after they were buried. Their son had been in the ground for days.

The man wrestled the monkey's paw from his wife and silently made the third and final wish. The wife reached the door and flung it open, but no one was there.

"I don't get it," Catie Trimble had complained. "The story just *ends* like that? What was the last wish?"

Natasha had needed no explanation. Neither had Stanley, who was in Natasha's English class.

"Think about it," Stanley had said. "The boy had *died*."

"Yeah, but his mom wished him back alive!"

"And her wish worked," Stanley had said patiently. "He came back to life."

"Which was a good thing," Catie had insisted. "I still don't get it."

Ms. Woodward, at the front of the room, had refrained from interfering.

"It wasn't a good thing because the boy had already been buried," Stanley had said. "It was his *body* that came back to life."

"Oh!" a guy named Erich had said. "He was rotten!"

140

"He probably had maggots all over him," another guy had said happily. "Plus, bodies stink when they decay. Like, really really bad."

Catie had turned pale and told the boys that they were just mean. That they were making fun of *all* wishes by turning them into something stupid and gross, and wasn't that freedom of religion, except the opposite? Wasn't it the *opposite* of freedom of religion? Catie was allowed to believe in wishes as much as she wanted, she'd exclaimed, and Stanley and Erich shouldn't get to make fun of her just because she got a Wishing Day and they didn't!

At that, Ms. Woodward had stepped in and said it was time to move on. Catie had sniffled for the rest of the hour, sending red-rimmed glares at anyone who looked at her.

It made Natasha wonder if Catie had had her Wishing Day already, and if so, what she'd wished for.

A few weeks later, Ms. Woodward made them read a poem called "The Second Coming." It was a shivery sort of poem, but in a good way. It was about how life was bigger and more unpredictable than anyone could grasp, kind of.

The last line had imprinted itself in Natasha's brain: "And what rough beast, its hour come round at last, slouches towards Bethlehem to be born?"

Catie Trimble had complained about "The Second Coming," too. Lots of kids had. Natasha's class echoed with the refrain of, "Why do we have to read this stuff? It's so *bo-o-o-oring*" and "How is this ever going to help us in the real world? It's not, that's how."

Stanley, Natasha remembered, had half raised his hand a couple of times and tried to talk about real things, like what he thought the poem meant and how he liked the way certain phrases sounded. He'd been shot down, and Natasha had sat there mutely.

She should have spoken up. The part about the beast had made her shudder, but it made her like the poem even more, because it meant the poem worked. If Natasha could ever make readers shudder or cry or laugh out loud, she would be ecstatic.

But stories and poems weren't real. They were made up.

If *Mama* came slouching home after all these years . . .

If Mama were dead, and Natasha's wish brought her back to life . . .

Natasha reached the stone bench that marked the halfway point of the trail. The bench was covered with snow, and Natasha imagined a woman lying beneath, her feet at one end and her head at the other. Her hands would be crossed over her chest, and her expression would be . . .

Oh, for heaven's sake, Natasha told herself, exasperated. *Her expression would be peaceful, okay? Can you stop being morbid, please?!*

She went two or three yards farther. She gazed at the lake, which had swallowed up a little kid two winters ago. The kid had run out onto the ice, and the ice broke beneath her.

Natasha wrapped her scarf more tightly around her. She hoped the Bird Lady *did* have a way to stay warm. She hoped the Bird Lady had a home, whatever form that home might take.

"Natasha!" Darya called.

Natasha blinked. She used her hand to shield her eyes from the sun and glanced all about.

"Natasha!"

She spotted Darya by the tree line, wearing a bright red coat and a frown. *Like Little Red Cap*, Natasha thought. *But grouchy.*

"It's time for dinner," Darya called, tromping closer. "Aunt Vera sent me to get you."

Natasha felt a strange falling sensation, similar to the other leaps out of time she'd experienced recently.

143

It couldn't be dinnertime. There was no way she'd been out here that long. She checked the horizon, and relief coursed through her.

"You're full of it," she told Darya. "The sun's just starting to set."

Darya picked her way through the final yards of high snow that separated them. She hadn't used the path. Instead, she'd taken a shortcut straight through the forest behind their house. She put her hands on her hips, and her body threw a hard shadow behind her.

"Fine," she said. "It's time for you to help *fix* dinner. Aunt Vera needs you to peel the potatoes."

"Why can't you peel the potatoes? Or Ava?" She gestured at Darya's feet. "And *flip-flops*, Darya? Really?"

"Boots are for wimps," Darya said. Her flip-flops were silver with narrow straps. Technically they were shoes, Natasha supposed. They compressed the snow the same way Natasha's sturdy boots did.

But Natasha's boots *covered her feet*.

Plus, Darya was wearing skinny jeans, and the snow reached the middle of her calves. The wet denim clung to her legs, and her feet looked pitiful at the bottom of the footstep-holes she'd made. Her toenails were painted blue, which was appropriate.

"You're going to get frostbite," Natasha said.

Darya shrugged. She had to be freezing, but if she didn't want to show it, she wouldn't.

She was also beautiful. She really really was. Natasha's face turned ruddy in the cold, but Darya's cheeks glowed, and her red hair shone with copper and golden highlights. Even scowling, she looked prettier than Natasha ever would.

Molly swore up and down that Natasha was wrong about the prettiness. Natasha was right about the popularity piece, Molly conceded, but that didn't matter because Natasha didn't want to be popular.

"I don't want to be pretty, either," Natasha had lied. "It's not my job to be pretty."

"No one said it was your *job*," Molly had said. They'd had this discussion late one summer evening, after watching a movie in which the beautiful girl (of course) ended up with the gorgeous guy. Molly had looked at Natasha half fondly, half with exasperation. "You can be pretty and still be whatever else you want to be."

"Molly. I'm not worried about this. I really don't care."

"I'm not saying you do. I'm just saying that you *are* pretty. Darya's flashier, and she knows how to work it.

That's why people notice her. And Ava's Ava, so . . ."
She'd shrugged, and Natasha's heart had swelled. Ava
was a shooting star. She was glad Molly saw it too.

"But Natasha," Molly had said. She'd put her hands
on Natasha's shoulders.

"Yes, Molly?" Natasha had replied, putting her
hands on Molly's shoulders.

"You. Are frickin'. Gorgeous. Darya is fire and
flame. You're dark and mysterious. Both are good."

Out by the lake, Natasha smiled.

"What?" Darya demanded.

"Nothing," Natasha said. Just, it had been nice of
Molly to say what she'd said. She hadn't thought of
that in ages.

"Okay, great," Darya said. "So what do you want
me to do? Go back and tell Aunt Vera to peel her damn
potatoes herself?"

Natasha laughed, imagining how that would go
over. She went to join her, crossing back past the stone
bench. On top of the mounded snow, resting in a small
indentation, was a note. It was folded in fourths. On the
uppermost side, just like the others, it said *Natasha*.

Holding it down was a clear blue marble as big as
an egg.

CHAPTER FOURTEEN

Natasha snatched the marble and the note and shoved both into her coat pocket.

Darya looked at her suspiciously. "What was that?"

"What was what?"

"You. Grabbing something off the bench."

"Don't know what you're talking about." Natasha plowed forward, reusing the footprints she'd already made.

Darya hurried to catch up, though she stayed behind Natasha rather than walking by her side.

"It was blue," Darya insisted. "The thing you grabbed."

Natasha felt Darya's hand on her coat, tugging at her pocket, and she whirled around and slapped Darya away.

"Quit it!" she said.

Darya drew back. She looked stung. "Quit it, or what?"

Natasha glared. Darya glared back. Darya clenched her hands by her sides, and Natasha realized she was doing the same thing.

Natasha exhaled. She tried to relax her jaw, her posture, her fingers. She breathed in slowly, one-two-three-four, then breathed out to the same count. The last thing she wanted to do was give Darya something to grip onto. Darya was as stubborn as a dog with a bone if she thought something was going on that she didn't know about.

"It was a piece of trash," Natasha said.

"No it wasn't," Darya said.

"Yes it was."

"Then show me."

Natasha started walking, her thoughts tumbling about. She wasn't going to show Darya the note. The note was hers. For the first time in a very long time, *she* was the one singled out as special.

Darya followed. Her flip-flops smacked against her heels, and Natasha knew she was making the sound as loud and annoying as possible. *Smack smack smack.* Natasha hoped Darya had snow between each and every toe. She hoped Darya *did* get frostbite—only not really.

Her fingers itched to ball up again.

She tried a trick that sometimes helped when she felt out of control. She imagined herself floating above her body, watching the scene from above. Two girls marching through the snow. One with a secret, the other determined to figure out what it was. If this were a story . . . if the two girls were characters in a book . . . what would happen next? How would the first girl twist the situation to her advantage?

She grounded herself back in reality. She smiled pleasantly, even though Darya was behind her and could only see the back of her head.

"You're right. It wasn't a piece of trash," she said. She laughed. "How do you always know these things? Has anyone *ever* been able to fool you, like in your entire life?"

"No," Darya said.

There were snow crunching sounds, and Natasha turned around.

Natasha looked over her shoulder. "Your poor feet. Do you at least want to wear my socks?"

She lifted one foot and tugged off her boot, hopping to keep her balance. She pulled off her sock and put her boot back on. She repeated the process with her other foot. She steadied herself by putting her hand on Darya's shoulder. Darya didn't shrug her off.

"Here," she said. She held out her warm, dry socks, which had unicorns on them. *Ironic* unicorns, she'd insisted to Molly when Molly saw them. "Whatever you say," Molly had replied.

Darya hesitated, then accepted the socks. She leaned against Natasha and put them on. She wedged the fabric between her big toe and her second toe to make them flip-flop friendly.

"Thanks," Darya said.

Natasha pulled the marble from her pocket, but left the note. She held it out and said, "It's Benton's."

"Why do you have it?" Darya asked. "Is it a marble?"

Natasha nodded.

"You stole Benton's marble."

"Borrowed," Natasha said.

"Why?"

"I don't know. Because?"

"Why did Benton have the marble in the first place?" Darya asked.

"Because boys keep the whole world in their pockets? I don't know. One day a teacher needed pliers, and Benton fished a pair out of his jeans." This detail was actually true. "He had a pair of pliers in his pocket."

"Weird," Darya said.

Natasha spotted Papa's workshop, and just beyond it, their house. Potatoes, Aunt Vera, homework . . . and a note in her pocket begging to be read.

She closed her fingers around the marble and put it back with the note.

"Do you have a crush on him?" Darya asked.

"Who?" Natasha said, hoping to buy some time.

Darya cocked her head.

Natasha swallowed. This was the make-it-or-break-it part of their exchange. Natasha did have a crush on Benton, but that was her business. Not Darya's.

On the other hand, the marble wasn't his, and Darya didn't know about the note. None of that was Darya's business, either.

So which did she give up? If she claimed not to have a crush on Benton, Darya would know she was lying, and a crack like that could bring the whole story down. Darya would return to hounding her about the contents of her pocket. She'd lunge and dodge and jab her pointy elbows until she managed to claim the note or break Natasha's ribs. Or both.

"I guess," she said reluctantly.

"You have a crush on Benton," Darya stated. "*You*. You have a crush on Benton!"

"You don't have to tell the whole world," Natasha said.

Darya waved her hand at the stretch of land around them. "Yeah, the squirrels are really going to care, if there are any out there. They're probably having tea in their little . . . squirrel holes."

She startled Natasha by coming to an abrupt halt, grinning widely, and taking Natasha's hands.

"Natasha!" she exclaimed. "You have a crush on Benton! That's awesome!"

"It is?" Natasha said. Darya was being nice, and Natasha felt guilty. Should she share more stuff with Darya in general? If she did, would Darya share stuff with her? Would they be better sisters?

The house was fifteen feet away. As soon as they got there, she would tell her aunt that she had to run up to her room before helping with dinner. Or that she had to go to the bathroom. Anything that would buy her a minute—a single minute! That was all she needed!—to read the note. Alone.

Darya opened the back door and yanked Natasha inside. "Found her!" she announced.

Aunt Vera turned from the stove. "Yes, I can see that," she said. "Let me guess—she was off with Emily, concocting all sorts of plans for the seventh-grade dance."

"What?" Darya said.

Natasha felt the world turn upside down.

"Who's *Emily*?" Darya asked. "And Natasha doesn't do dances."

Aunt Vera stood dumbly. "She . . . I . . . did I say Emily? I don't know any Emilys."

"Then you need to lay off the vodka, because you're too young to be having senior moments," Darya said. "And you're sweating. If your sweat drips into the soup, I am *not* eating it."

"Hi, Natasha," Ava said, skipping into the kitchen. She dropped down at the table, plunking her drawing pad and a collection of pens in front of her. "I'm making blueprints for my dream house. Want to see?"

Aunt Elena followed on Ava's heels with a stack of neatly folded dishcloths. "Vera, good heavens, you look like you're about to faint," she said.

Aunt Vera came out of her trance. She blinked and said, "Maybe I am. Maybe *you* should try standing over a hot stove while *I* watch a silly soap opera and fold the laundry." She turned her attention to Darya. "And I do *not* drink vodka, young lady."

Aunt Elena noticed Darya and Natasha. She gaped at Darya's feet and said, "Darya! You did *not* wear flip-flops out in the snow. Tell me you didn't wear flip-flops in the snow!"

Darya flashed Aunt Elena a smile. "Okay. I didn't wear flip-flops in the snow."

Aunt Elena pointed at the staircase. "Go change. Now. And soak your feet in hot water!"

"After I change or before?"

"You too, Natasha," Aunt Elena said. "Get those boots off, and your coat. Put all your things in the mudroom."

"Then come right back," Aunt Vera said. "I can't make mashed potatoes if the potatoes don't get peeled, now can I?"

"No," Natasha said. "I mean yes. Yes to the potatoes, yes to the mudroom. Yes to the yes things and no to the no things."

Ava looked at her funny. "Natasha, what's wrong?

Do you need to use the bathroom?"

Natasha's cheeks grew warm.

Darya slooshed off her wet socks, and Aunt Elena scolded her for getting water on the floor.

"You're the one who told me to take them off!" Darya protested.

"In the mudroom!" Aunt Elena exclaimed.

Natasha slipped away. She took off her boots like a good girl. She took off her coat and hung it up where it belonged. *Such* a good girl. She tiptoed to the staircase, scurried to her room, and locked the door.

She perched on the edge of her bed and opened her left hand. The blue marble was like a piece of the sky. She opened her right hand. The note was slightly damp in her palm. The handwriting and the way it was folded was exactly like the others.

CHAPTER FIFTEEN

Natasha had time to read the note exactly once before Darya burst in triumphantly, wiggling an Allen wrench in the air.

"Ah-ha!" Darya crowed. "Bet you forgot this trick, didn't you?"

"Darya!" She clutched the note to her chest. "What are you doing? Get out!"

Darya sauntered to Natasha's bed and dropped down beside her. She tossed the Allen wrench onto Natasha's nightstand. "You don't always trust me, you know."

"Are you kidding me? Are you kidding me right

now?" Natasha said. She kept the note pressed to her chest. She wanted to move it, to sit on it or hide it or put it in her pocket, but she didn't want Darya to notice.

"*You just broke into my room,*" she said. "Why in the world *should* I trust you?"

Darya eyed the note. She lifted her gaze to Natasha's.

Natasha shoved the note under her thigh. "Go. Away."

Darya leaned back on her forearms. She straightened her legs and wiggled her toes, which were now covered by blue socks with penguins on them. "I borrowed another pair of your socks from the mudroom. They're cute. Can I keep them?"

"Darya—" Natasha's voice jumped in the way of almost crying. It surprised her.

It surprised Darya, too. She sat up straight and said, "What is it? What's going on, for real?"

Natasha shook her head. Everything seemed too big. Too much. She refolded the note with sharp, angry movements and gave it to Darya. *Why not?*

Darya stared at Natasha for a long moment. Natasha didn't trust herself to speak.

Darya placed the note between them on the bed.

She didn't open it. "Natasha, I'm not out to get you. But I'm your *sister.* Doesn't that count for anything?"

Natasha shrugged. When they were younger, Darya had idolized Natasha. Natasha, in return, had been a *really good* big sister. She included Darya in stuff. She made her laugh. She watched out for her, and she *never* teased her, not in an unkind way.

They'd grown apart, though. Eventually Darya had wanted to be more than just Natasha's adoring little sister; maybe that was what started it. She'd wanted to be her own person—the gall! Natasha had known her reaction was ridiculous, but she'd felt rejected. Darya had found her own circle of friends. Maybe she liked them more than she liked Natasha.

So Natasha had pulled away too, out of pride. At home, Natasha began paying more attention to Ava than Darya, and when Darya brought it up, she'd pretended not to understand.

"We can't leave her out just because she's littler," she'd told Darya.

"I'm not saying we should!" Darya had said. "I just . . . I miss *us.* Don't you?"

"I'm right here," Natasha had replied coolly. "*I* haven't gone anywhere."

Darya's face had crumpled, and Natasha had

158

shrugged and turned away.

"Hey, Ava," she'd called. "Want to play Slap Jack?"

Natasha had done that. For the first time in her life, she'd hurt Darya's feelings on purpose.

The distance between Natasha and Darya had plenty of other causes. Both sisters allowed it to grow. But when Natasha looked at Darya now, she felt a great hole of regret.

A tear, and then another, trickled down her cheek.

"Natasha, shhh," Darya said, putting her arm around Natasha and pulling her close. She stroked Natasha's hair.

"Did something bad happen?" Darya asked. "Does it have to do with Benton? Did you honestly steal his marble?"

Natasha hitch-laughed. "It's not his. Or it might be, I don't know. I don't know whose it is." She pulled back and swiped at her eyes. "Or, wow. Maybe it's Aunt Elena's."

"From when she was little? The one the Bird Lady supposedly gave her?"

Natasha was astonished. "She told *you* that story? When?"

"A long time ago," Darya said. "Let me see it again."

Natasha gave her the marble. Darya held it up to the light and turned it this way and that. She shook her head definitively and said, "Nope, not hers."

She tossed it to Natasha, whose fingers closed around it as if they'd been created for that very purpose.

"How do you know?" Natasha asked.

"It's round."

"So?"

"Aunt Elena's was shaped like an egg, a blue glass egg."

"But mine's the *size* of an egg."

"And my eyeball is the size of your eyeball." Darya made an impatient sound. "A blue glass egg, that's how she described it. A blue glass egg that Aunt Elena probably made up, but a blue. Glass. *Egg.*" She jerked her chin at the marble. "Would you describe that as an egg?"

"It's blue . . ."

"Lots of things are blue." Darya drew her whole body onto the bed and sat cross-legged. She adjusted her feet until her toes were tucked beneath her knees. "Can I read the note?"

Natasha bit her lip, then nodded.

Darya picked it up and unfolded it. Her eyes moved across the paper. She lifted her head and asked, "What does it mean?"

Natasha leaned over and retrieved the other two notes from beneath her bed, where they'd lain smooth and flat between the pages of her journal. She passed them to Darya.

Darya read each one aloud.

"'You don't know how special you are. Lots of people don't know how special you are. But I do. And you are.'"

She put that one to the side.

"'You don't know how beautiful you are, either.'" Darya glanced up. Natasha shrugged. Darya returned to the note. "'You should smile more, Natasha. When you smile, it lights up your face.'"

She placed that one with the other. She lifted the most recent note and read it aloud: "'Would you like to talk?'"

She set it down. She studied Natasha. "So?"

"So," Natasha repeated.

"You either have a stalker or a secret admirer. Or both." Darya put all three notes together, tapped them against her thigh, and returned the stack to Natasha. "*Do* you want to talk to him?"

"If they're from Benton, then yes," she said. She bunched her bedspread in her hand. "But what if they're not? And what would I say to him?"

"Hmm," Darya said. "Just to be clear—you swear you didn't write them yourself, right?"

"Darya!"

Darya arched her eyebrows. "Maybe you wrote them yourself and didn't even know it. Maybe you have a split personality."

Natasha revised her opinion of Darya's new and caring personality. She picked up her notes, rose from the bed, and said, "I've totally got a split personality. You nailed it. And now would you *please leave*, like I've been asking you to all along?"

"Wait. I take it back."

"Too late," Natasha said stiffly.

Darya uncrossed her legs and stood up. "Okay, let me think. The notes *could* be from Benton. It's possible. He's not going out with anybody, and he travels between crowds, if you know what I mean."

"No," Natasha said.

"Sometimes he hangs out with the popular kids, sometimes he hangs out with the jocks." She pinned Natasha with her stare. "He's friends with nerdy kids, too."

"Like me? I'm nerdy?"

"Duh. And Stanley, his best friend."

Natasha walked across her room and opened

her door. She wasn't rude. She wasn't defensive. (She hoped.) She just stood by her door and waited.

Darya rolled her eyes. "Have you told Ava? You should tell Ava. She's twelve now, you know."

"Why yes, I do."

"And she's sneaky, so she's good at figuring out other people's sneakiness."

"Thanks for your input. Bye."

Darya took her own sweet time strolling from the bed to the door. "Next weekend is the Spring Festival. Everyone will be there—we can hunt down Benton and, like, watch him."

"Awesome plan. You should be a detective."

Darya reached Natasha and paused. They were the same height, but not for long, Natasha feared. Soon Darya would be taller than she was.

"I think it's cool," Darya said. "I wish someone would leave me secret love notes."

Natasha started to reply, but stopped.

"What are you going to tell him?" Darya asked. "Yes, you want to talk, or no, you don't? And *how* are you going to tell him?"

Natasha felt ill. She had no idea.

"You could wear a shirt, maybe. We could use a Sharpie and write 'yes' or 'no' across it?"

"No thank you," Natasha said faintly.

"Regardless, we need to stake out the scene *together*—you, me, and Ava—just in case the notes are from a stalker. I don't think they are, because they didn't give me a bad feeling. They didn't send off warning vibes, you know?"

Warning vibes? Stake out the scene? Darya would never talk like this in front of her friends. But here she was, talking exactly like this to Natasha.

"*Ohhh,*" Darya said.

"What?" Natasha said.

"What about Molly? You're probably going to the Spring Festival with Molly." She looked disappointed, but tried to cover it up. "What does Molly think about the notes?"

"I haven't told her."

"You haven't?"

"I don't know *why* I haven't. I just . . . haven't. I probably should, huh?"

"Up to you," Darya said neutrally.

"Molly's great," Natasha said, all of a sudden feeling like a jerk.

"I know she is."

"It's just, sometimes, she can be a little judgy."

"I've never seen her be judgy."

Natasha twisted the fingers of one hand with her other hand. Nothing about this conversation was going how Natasha would have thought.

"But it doesn't matter, because Molly isn't going to the Spring Festival," she told Darya. "She's—"

Natasha frowned. Molly wouldn't be at the Spring Festival because . . . *ugh*. Why wouldn't Molly be at the Spring Festival again?

"Her cousin's bar mitzvah!" she exclaimed. "She's going to her cousin's bar mitzvah with her parents. She's going to be out of town for the whole weekend."

"Huh," Darya said.

"Yeah," Natasha said, feeling even more like a jerk. Molly had told Natasha all about the bar mitzvah, and getting to go shopping to find a new outfit, and how she hoped her cousin's cute friend would be there. His name was Mason or Curtis, something like that. How had Natasha spaced that out?

Darya flipped her hair over her shoulders and shook her head so that her curls fell just the way she wanted. "All right, then. I'm glad we had this little chat. On Saturday, we'll go to the Festival."

She strolled out of the room. From the hall, she turned back.

"Does this by any chance have to do with your

Wishing Day wishes?" Darya asked.

Natasha grew flustered. "You don't believe in Wishing Day wishes. You don't believe in magic, period."

"Never said I did."

"Then why does it matter?"

Darya regarded Natasha with what looked an awful lot like pity. "Because *you* do."

CHAPTER SIXTEEN

It didn't take long for Darya to share the news about the notes with Ava. Darya dismissed the notion that magic was involved, however, since she dismissed the notion that magic existed. She insisted that Natasha simply hadn't seen whoever left her the notes.

"Exactly," Natasha argued over Monday night's dinner. Aunt Vera was playing bridge at a neighbor's house. Aunt Elena had gone to the movies, she'd said, though she grew pink and couldn't come up with an answer when Darya asked her what she was seeing. Natasha assumed she simply wanted a night off, and she didn't blame her.

Papa sat at the head of the table, spooning vegetable soup into his mouth and letting their conversation swirl around him.

"I didn't *see* anyone because there wasn't anyone to *see*," Natasha said. "Let's play a game of pretend, 'kay?"

"Enh," Darya said.

"You girls, with your imagination games," Papa said. He exhaled. "Klara had such an imagination. When you were younger, she'd get right down on the floor and play with you. Sometimes she was a queen, sometimes a king. Sometimes a donkey!"

"That's funny, Papa," Ava said.

"She had an invisible friend when she was a girl. I didn't know her then, not really, but I heard about her later, Klara's invisible friend." His eyes focused sharply and landed on Natasha. "Emily. That was her name. And she looked like you, Natasha. Klara said so once."

Natasha's blood reversed directions in her veins. "N-no, Papa, I don't think so."

"Imaginary friend, you mean," Darya said. She tore off a second piece of bread. "An *invisible* friend— now that would actually be cool."

Natasha bowed her head. She placed her hands on the table to steady herself.

Darya passed Papa the breadbasket. "Here, Papa. Have some more bread." She looked quizzically at Natasha. "You said we were going to play a game of pretend."

"You said 'enh,'" Natasha croaked.

"So?"

Lots of people have brown hair and brown eyes, Natasha told Papa silently. *You have brown hair and brown eyes. Everyone says I look like you, you know.*

"Hey," Darya said. She snapped her fingers in Natasha's face.

Natasha blinked several times and took a long sip of milk. Her dizziness passed.

"Well . . . okay . . . look down," she told Darya. "Do you see your fork?"

"Yes, because we're having soup, which means we don't need forks. There mine is, clean as a whistle."

"That expression doesn't make sense," Natasha said.

"*You* don't make sense."

"Ha ha. Now watch." Natasha grabbed Darya's fork. "Did you see me take your fork?"

"Nope," Darya said.

"You did, too!" Ava said.

"Natasha, give Darya back her fork," Papa said.

"Yes, Papa," Natasha said. "Darya, here's your fork."

"Cool. Thanks. Not that I *need* it . . ."

"But guess what?"

"What?"

"Those two seconds it took me to steal your fork?"

"Girls, don't steal each other's silverware," Papa said.

"That's how long it took each note to appear. If someone had *been* there, I would have seen them."

"Enh," Darya said again. "You get lost in your thoughts sometimes, like someone else we know." She jerked her chin at Papa, who was gazing into his empty soup bowl.

"She's not *that* bad," Ava said. She patted Papa's hand. "No offense, Papa."

"Hmm?" Papa said. "No, no offense taken."

"Thank you, Ava," Natasha said. "And I'm sorry for not telling you myself. I would have. Darya just got to you first."

"A whole day later," Darya commented.

"Ava, Darya is being annoying on purpose. Ignore her."

"Or just *pretend* to ignore me," Darya said. "Pretend you don't see me, like Natasha pretended not to

see her *secret admirer person of mystery.*" That last
bit, she whispered loudly.

She reverted to her normal voice. "Which brings
up an intriguing point. We think Benton left the notes,
right? Or we hope he did."

"Darya, not now," Natasha said.

"Oh, whatever. Papa doesn't care." She turned to
Papa. "We love you, Papa."

"We really do," Ava said.

Papa's eyes teared up. "And I love you girls. So, so
much."

Darya got back to the task at hand. "But Natasha.
If Benton left the notes, and yet Benton was *invisible*
or whatever . . ." She spread her hands, palms up.
"How's that supposed to work? Is Benton *your* invisible friend?"

Natasha stood. She collected her bowl, Papa's bowl,
and her sisters' bowls. She took them from the table to
the sink, and she grabbed the cake dish from the counter on her return trip. She'd made a buttermilk fudge
cake, because Papa liked it. It was moist and crumbly
and thick with frosting.

Ava tugged her arm when she came back, before
she sat down. "I believe in magic. You know I do."

"Thanks, Ava," Natasha said.

"And I think the you-know-whats could have been written by you-know-who and *delivered* magically. Or something."

"You don't need to talk in code," Darya said.

"*Darya,*" Natasha said, irritated. Yes, Papa was out of it. No, that wasn't news to anyone, even to Ava. But he was still Papa. He deserved their respect.

"Sorry," Darya muttered. She glanced at Papa. "Sorry, Papa."

"It's all right, just don't do it again," Papa said automatically.

"I mean, no one ever said that boys don't have magic," Ava went on.

"They don't," Darya said.

"We don't know that for sure," Ava said. "We don't know anything for sure."

Natasha stood across from Ava, holding the cake plate. "You know, that's kind of true."

"I tried telling you-know-who that"—Ava rolled her eyes and pointed to Darya—"but she wouldn't listen."

"Tell me what?" Papa said.

All three girls swiveled their heads to look at him.

"Oh!" Ava exclaimed, turning red. "Papa, I didn't . . . I didn't mean—"

"That Darya's decided to eat more healthily,"

172

Natasha said. "That's what Ava didn't tell you." She bypassed Darya in her loop around the table, lifting the cake plate up and over her head. "No buttermilk fudge cake for her, which means Ava gets double."

"Yay!" Ava said.

"*Hey!*" Darya protested.

"You're the one who said you didn't need your fork," Natasha said.

Papa looked confused.

⁓

After cleaning up the dinner dishes, Natasha went to her bedroom. She lay on her bed, tummy down and elbows propped up, and wrote a story about a shy girl and a very cute boy. The shy girl didn't think the cute boy ever noticed her, but he did, and at their fall formal, he found her in the shadows and asked her to dance. He picked *her* over all the other girls.

He took her hand and led her to the middle of the gym, she wrote.

Dots of light flickered over them, and Delilah thought about fireflies, and the smell of rain, and how strong Pete's hand felt on the small of her back.

He pulled her closer. "I'm going to kiss you now," he said. "Okay?"

Delilah felt dizzy. Was this actually happening, or was it a dream?

"Yes," she whispered. "Okay."

His lips brushed hers, and every doubt fell away. Pete was real, the dance was real, the kiss was real. None of it would disappear.

Coming out of the story was like coming up for air. She felt dizzy, just like Delilah. Just like she had when Papa mentioned the name *Emily*—although Natasha didn't want to dwell on that.

Then the knowledge of what she'd done sunk in.

She picked up her pen.

THE END, she wrote in big block letters, because she'd done it. For the first time in her life, she had finished a story. It had a beginning! And a middle! AND AN ENDING!

Her elation lasted for five minutes, a blaze of pride and accomplishment.

Then it died down, but a small, steady flame remained.

It was possible her story sucked. It probably did. *But she'd done it.* She'd started a story and made it all the way to the end.

CHAPTER SEVENTEEN

B right and early the following Saturday, Ava twirled in the snow, her head thrown back and her arms widespread. Natasha watched her from the back door, her fingertips lightly touching the cold panes of the windows built into the frame.

The morning sun highlighted Ava's cheekbones and small, straight nose. Her pale brown hair held hints of Darya's red, which the sun picked up as well. The sun loved Ava, and Ava loved the sun.

Ava loved everything, fiercely and unself-consciously. Like the twirling. Ava twirled for the joy of it, Natasha could tell. She twirled to say thank you to the universe for the snow and the sky, for mittens and magic and warm winter boots.

When had Natasha last twirled like that?

She twisted the doorknob and stepped outside. "Ava," she said.

Ava stopped spinning. She stumbled and laughed. "Natasha! Good morning! You're finally up!"

"Finally?!" Natasha said. It was barely eight a.m.

"Yeah, silly, because today's the day of the Spring Festival! Aren't you so excited?"

"Maybe, but it doesn't start this early. And I'm not silly."

Ava looked at her funny. "Okay. Are you grumpy? Why are you grumpy?"

"I'm not," Natasha said, feeling herself blush.

She crossed the crunchy snow of the yard and went to the swing Papa had made for them long ago. The seat was a bench-like plank of cedar, three feet wide and eight inches deep. It hung from two thickly braided ropes, which Papa had thrown over a tree limb that was at least twenty feet from the ground. It was the most awesome swing ever.

When the sisters were smaller, they'd swung on it two at a time, which required scrunching close together and looping their arms over each other's shoulders so that both girls could hang on tight to both ropes. Natasha remembered swinging side by side with Mama, too. That had been a long time ago, but she could still call up the feeling, like a flying hug.

Natasha flipped the seat to dump off the snow and ice. She flipped it back, wiped it dry with her glove, and sat down. She took hold of the ropes and nudged herself back and forth with the toe of her boot.

She made a conscious effort to lighten her tone, saying, "Anyway, Darya's still sleeping like a log. How long have *you* been up?"

Ava came over. Her hat had a pom-pom on it. Her cheeks were little apples. "Six-thirty? Maybe seven? It was still dark outside, so probably more in the six-ish range."

"Why so early?" Natasha asked.

"It's the weekend. I want to soak up every last drop of it." She propped one knee on the swing and gripped the rope closest to her with both hands, which made the swing list sideways.

"Hey," Natasha protested.

"Mama used to love this swing," Ava said, her breath warm.

"How do you know? You were three when she left."

Ava chided her with a look. "Papa told me. And

just because I was three doesn't mean I don't remember *any*thing about Mama. I remember lots of stuff. Like, something about a snail, and a mouse, and—" She twisted her mouth. "Do you remember something about a snail and a mouse? A rhyme-y kind of thing?"

Natasha did. She was floored that Ava did. "Slowly, slowly, very slowly, crept the little snail," she said.

"Slowly, slowly, very slowly, up the garden trail," Ava said.

"But quickly, quickly, very quickly, ran the little mouse . . ." Natasha passed it over to Ava, but Ava wrinkled her forehead, so Natasha finished for her. "Quickly, quickly, very quickly, all around the house!"

She ended the rhyme by tickling Ava's stomach, because that's how it worked. Ava smiled a bit remotely.

Natasha gave her a moment. Then she said, "So Papa says Mama liked to swing?"

"Uh-huh. Papa says she asked him to make the rope swing for us, but really she was the one who wanted it. I guess it was kind of a joke between them, since she was a grown-up and not a kid."

"Oh," Natasha said. "Papa told you that?"

"He says I'm like her, because I smile so much. But she didn't *always* smile."

"Well, neither do you."

"Yeah, but . . ." She released the swing, pushing off it with her knee and stepping back. Natasha clutched the ropes more tightly, reacting to the shift in balance.

"Why did she leave, Natasha? Do you know?"

Natasha shook her head. "Nobody does."

Ava folded her arms across her chest. She stared into the distance.

"Papa's teaching me how to make a lute," she said, and maybe Natasha was wrong, but she thought she heard a hint of wistfulness in her voice.

"Cool," Natasha said.

"He'll teach you, too," Ava said quickly. "He wants to, you and Darya both. But he thinks you're not, um . . ."

"I'm not," Natasha said, laughing. When Ava didn't join in, she drew her eyebrows together. "Ava, I'm *glad* he's teaching you. At least one of his daughters is interested!"

Ava looked relieved. "Today, at the Festival, I'm going to help him at his booth, but not until after we find Benton."

"Benton might not be the one leaving the notes. We don't know for sure."

"We'll figure it out," Ava said confidently, and Natasha sensed that whatever shadow had fallen over her—*if* a shadow had fallen over her, if Natasha hadn't just made it up—was gone.

"Ava?"

"Yeah?"

"Do you ever get sad? Or grumpy or grouchy or anything?"

Ava took the question seriously. "Hmm. I guess I don't see the point in feeling any of those ways. What good does it do?"

"But feelings are feelings. They aren't something you choose."

"Aren't they?"

"Not for me," Natasha said. "I mean, I hide what I'm feeling sometimes. Lots of times. But I *feel* whatever it is just the same."

"Well, I guess I do too," Ava admitted. "I just . . . I don't think it's fair. To other people. To get sad all the time, you know?"

Natasha wondered how much Papa shared with Ava during their lute-making sessions. Had he told Ava about Mama's "dark times," and that when Mama got sad, it was a deeper sort of sadness than most people felt?

She hopped off the swing and went to Ava. "Hey,

Ava? I don't *want* you to be sad, but it's all right if you are."

"But I'm not."

"Good. But everybody gets sad sometimes. And there's a difference between normal-sad and sad-sad, if that makes sense."

"It does. And I wasn't saying that *you* do that, about being sad around other people."

Natasha was startled. "Um, okay. Good."

"Anyway, the notes make you happy, right?"

"Sure," Natasha said. "Yes."

Ava looked at Natasha. Then her gaze moved to something just past her. Her eyes widened, and a smile stretched across her face. "Then be happy! On the swing, where you just were. See?!"

Natasha glanced back, and her heart skipped a beat. Tucked into the knot connecting the rope to the seat was something small, square, and flat. It was white. It was folded into fourths. On the top was a single word: *Natasha*.

CHAPTER EIGHTEEN

Natasha looked right and left, craning to spot the person who left it. Because Natasha had been right here this whole time, she and Ava both.

"Ava, did you see who put this here?" Natasha asked.

Ava shook her head.

"Was it here earlier? When you were twirling, before I came outside?"

"I don't think so," Ava said. She considered. "Or . . . I guess *maybe* it could have been. I didn't have my eyeballs glued to the swing. But Natasha, you swang on the swing."

"Swung," Natasha said.

"Swung. Did *you* see it, when you first sat down?"

"Definitely not," Natasha said. She gazed into the trees around them. "What about an old lady? Did you see an old lady wandering around, maybe?"

"An old lady?"

"Yeah. In a yellow raincoat?"

Ava furrowed her brow.

"Did you hear anything?" Natasha pressed. "Like footsteps, or twigs cracking?"

"No-o-o-o . . ." Ava said. "Why in a yellow rain-coat?"

Natasha pressed her fingers to the bridge of her nose. "Never mind."

Ava went to the swing and grabbed the note. She held it by one corner, as if preparing to shake it open. "May I?"

"I guess," Natasha said hesitantly. Then, "No! I mean, it's got my name on it, so maybe I'm supposed to be the one to open it."

"So open it."

Natasha hesitated. What if this note proved that Benton wasn't the one who'd been writing them? "I don't know if I want to."

"Of course you do," Ava said.

Natasha went to her, and Ava held out the note. Her eyes held curiosity and excitement, nothing more, and Natasha felt relieved. She wasn't the only one who saw notes where no notes had been before.

But her mouth was dry, so she said, "Go ahead. You can be the one."

"Are you sure?"

Natasha nodded. Fair or unfair, with Ava she *was* sure.

Ava unfolded the note and read it out loud:

"'Hope' is the thing with feathers
That perches in the soul
And sings the tune without the words
And never stops at all."

Ava lowered the note. "Aw," she said. "That's nice."

"It's from a poem we read in English," Natasha said. Her heart jumped. "Benton's not in my class, but all the seventh graders read the same stuff! But what does it mean?"

"That you should be hopeful!" Ava exclaimed. "And have feathers! And never stop singing!"

"That's not very helpful," Natasha said.

"*Hope*ful, not *help*ful." Ava grinned. "Did that help?"

"Actually, no."

Ava refolded the note and gave it to Natasha. "It means that Benton is *hoping* you'll find him," she said. "And talk to him, and dance around the Maypole with him!"

Natasha imagined herself dancing with Benton and went wobbly. She put the note in her pocket and said, "There's not going to be a Maypole."

"The *March* pole, then. Picky, picky." She looped her arm through Natasha's and led her to the house. "I'll wake up Darya if she isn't already up. You should eat some oatmeal or something. You look pale. We don't want you fainting at the Festival."

Was *Ava* taking care of *her*? Wasn't it supposed to be the other way around?

And Darya. Last weekend Darya had hugged Natasha when Natasha was crying. She'd taken care of Natasha, too.

Both of her sisters had the ability to help her—and the willingness. Was it possible they always had?

"Should we tell the aunts?" Ava asked.

Natasha halted. She locked her knees. "Tell them *what?*"

"Kidding! Natasha, I'm kidding," Ava said. The cold air hung between them. Ava patted Natasha's shoulder. She stroked the length of Natasha's arm. "It's going to be all right. You're not going to faint."

Natasha was struck with a dreadful thought. *Hope is the thing with feathers.* Birds had feathers. What if the Bird Lady . . . ?

No, she thought. *Please. Let the notes be from anyone but the Bird Lady.*

Ava escorted Natasha into the kitchen. She took Natasha's coat, hat, and gloves off. She guided Natasha to the stove and said, "Oatmeal?" She grinned. "Ple-e-a-a-se?"

"Hold on," Natasha said. "You want me to fix *you* oatmeal? I thought we were talking about me!"

"You can have a bowl, too."

"You are *so* generous," Natasha said. "Wow."

"You're welcome," Ava said.

Natasha shook her head, but she didn't really mind. She filled a pot with water and put it on the stove. She struck a match and lit the burner.

Ava kicked off her boots and shrugged out of her coat. She took a seat at the kitchen table, put her hands behind her head, and propped her feet on the chair across from her. She had appropriated a pair of Natasha's socks just like Darya had. This pair had kittens on them, and Natasha had been wondering where they'd gone. Unbelievable.

"Listen," Ava said. "Getting notes from a secret admirer is *awesome*, Natasha. Not scary, but awesome. 'Kay?"

Natasha went to the pantry and got out the Quaker Oats. "What if he's not there?"

"Who?"

"Benton."

"Where?"

"At the Festival!"

"Oh," Ava said. She sounded unconcerned. "He will be."

"What if he's not?"

"Then we'll have a caramel apple," Ava said. "You like caramel apples."

Natasha nodded. She did.

"See?" Ava said. "Sisters are for trusting. So trust me! Everything's going to work out fine."

CHAPTER NINETEEN

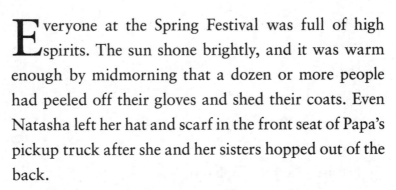

Everyone at the Spring Festival was full of high spirits. The sun shone brightly, and it was warm enough by midmorning that a dozen or more people had peeled off their gloves and shed their coats. Even Natasha left her hat and scarf in the front seat of Papa's pickup truck after she and her sisters hopped out of the back.

While Ava helped Papa set up his booth, Darya fixed Natasha's windblown hair, tucking some strands behind her ears and teasing others out. Natasha shook out Darya's handiwork the moment Darya moved on to fixing and fluffing Natasha's outfit. Natasha didn't know what Darya was hoping to accomplish, given that she was wearing jeans, a sweater, and her boring winter coat. How much fixing and fluffing did jeans and a winter coat require?

"There," Darya said, giving the bottom of Natasha's coat a final tug. "Ready?" she called to Ava.

Ava held out a thumbs-up. She kissed Papa's cheek and threaded her way through the maze of booths.

"Have fun, girls," Papa called to all of them.

"We will," they called back. "You, too!"

Ava took the lead, striding toward a crowd of kids by the cotton candy machine. "Boys. This way. I'm not sure they're the right boys—"

"The right *boy*," Darya corrected. "We're only looking for one boy, singular."

"Whatever," Ava said. "There can be one boy in a crowd of lots of boys, can't there?"

There could, and there was, and Natasha's stomach knotted up when she saw Benton (singular) standing next to the cotton candy machine. He had on faded jeans and a black leather jacket, and his black motorcycle boots had chains on the heels. He was adorable.

He lobbed peanuts at Dave Smith, and Dave Smith wrestled for the brown paper bag they came in. Natasha heard lots of *dude*s and *no frickin' way*s, along

189

with plenty of words they'd get in trouble for if they said them at school.

It was all very intimidating, and Natasha wished, suddenly, that Molly were there. She was grateful that Darya and Ava were with her, but Molly knew Natasha in a different way—and Molly was good at this stuff. Good at knowing how to help Natasha relax.

Molly would . . . oh, what *would* Molly do? Grab the bag of peanuts herself and dump them on Natasha's head?

Picking peanut shells out of her hair would be a distraction, that was true.

"Which one is he?" Ava asked.

"The cute one," Natasha said. It came out tiny.

"The one in the leather jacket and the embarrassing boots," Darya said.

Natasha looked at her indignantly.

"What?" Darya said. "They've got chains on them. *Chains.* And I'm pretty sure he doesn't ride a motorcycle, given that he's in seventh grade."

Natasha opened her mouth, then snapped it shut. But it was possible Benton owned a motorcycle, or had ridden one, or admired one from very close up. Darya didn't know everything.

"I like his hair," Ava pronounced.

"Me too," Natasha said.

"Too much product," Darya said.

Again, Natasha longed for Molly.

"Why are you being like this?" she said to Darya. "I thought you were excited for me. I thought you wanted me, you know, to like Benton and for him to maybe possibly like me back."

"I do," Darya said. "I can want all that and still mock him, can't I?"

"But you don't *have* to."

"Sorry," Darya muttered. "Maybe I'm jealous, okay?"

Natasha couldn't process what her sister just said. *CANNOT COMPUTE*, her brain informed her, and then she was moving forward. One step, two steps, three steps, because Ava had her by one arm and Darya had her by the other. Darya was talking, but Natasha's brain had yet to catch up. It made no sense that Darya could *ever* be jealous of *her*.

"So blah blah something something something," Darya finished. "Got it?"

"Huh?" Natasha said. They were only a few feet from Benton and his friends. She tried to dig her heels into the slushy snow.

Ava groaned. "Natasha. They are humans and we

191

are humans, and we are going to *talk* to them. You, especially, are going to talk to them. To Benton. And just be yourself, because you're wonderful."

Natasha shot a panicked look at Darya, who grinned wickedly.

"Hi," Ava said, planting herself smack-dab in front of the group of boys. She stuck out her hand and shook hands with them one by one: Stanley, Benton, and both Daves.

"I'm Ava," she said to each boy in turn. "Nice to meet you."

The Daves laughed.

"Uh, sure," Dave Winters said. "Whatever you say."

When Ava got to Stanley, Stanley shook her hand and said, "Hi, Ava. I'm Stanley."

"Nice to meet you," Ava said.

"Nice to meet you, too," Stanley said.

Dave Smith and Dave Winters cracked up. Benton did too.

"Boys," Darya scolded them, and they stopped clowning around. Natasha was amazed at Darya's ability to radiate confidence and scorn at the same time, and in such a way that it made boys like her more than they already did.

She had no reason to be jealous of Natasha, ever.

Darya gathered her hair into a temporary ponytail, then let her curls spill down her back. "Hi, Benton."

"Darya," Benton said with a grin.

"Aren't you going to say hi to Natasha?" Darya said.

Natasha was mortified, but Benton didn't appear to notice.

"Natasha, hi," he said, turning his attention to her. He stepped closer. "Hey, can I ask you a question?"

Natasha almost looked over her shoulder to see who he was really talking to, but she reined in the impulse.

"Me?" she squeaked. "Why?"

Darya elbowed her and gave her a hard stare.

"Because you're a girl," Benton said.

The Daves loved this and had all sorts of funny things to say, only they weren't nearly as funny as they thought they were.

"Shut up, idiots," Darya told them.

"Yeah," Benton said. To Natasha, he added, "And because you're not as scary as your sister."

"Darya or the little one?" Dave Smith said.

"Excuse me?" Darya said.

Dave held up his hands and said, "Sorry, sorry!"

Benton stepped away from the other guys. He led Natasha to a spot where the Daves couldn't hear, and Stanley, Darya, and Ava followed behind. "What I want to know is probably going to sound dumb, but . . ." He rubbed the back of his neck. "What if there's this girl you like. Or not a girl—for you it would be a boy—but pretend there's someone you like. Okay?"

Ava covered her mouth. This time, Darya elbowed her.

"Okay," Natasha said. She felt light-headed.

Benton jammed his hands in his pockets. "Just, what would you do?"

His leather jacket smelled good, like oil and dirt. His brown eyes were earnest. Benton on his own was less rowdy than Benton in a Big Group of Guys.

"I'd . . . tell her?" Natasha said.

"I've tried that already. Kind of."

"And she didn't do anything?" Darya asked.

Benton shook his head.

"Have you told her face-to-face?" Ava piped up. "Just flat out that you like her?"

"No," Benton said.

"He's worried she won't say it back," Stanley contributed.

She will! Natasha thought, but she couldn't say the

words if her life depended on it. Her throat was so tight she could barely breathe.

"You could write her a poem," Ava said innocently. "Or, you wouldn't even have to write it yourself. You could pick out a poem you liked and give it to her."

Confusion swept across Benton's face. "A poem?"

"Yeah," Ava said. "Everyone likes poems."

"I don't," Benton said. "Poems are crap."

"Poems aren't crap," Stanley said. "Not all of them."

"Dude. I'm not writing Belinda a poem." Benton turned to Natasha. "You wouldn't want some guy sending you a *poem*, would you?"

Natasha blinked hard.

"Wait. Is *Belinda* the girl you like?" Darya asked Benton.

"Who told you that?" Benton said, his eyes darting at the Daves.

"You did, just now," Stanley said. "Yes, he likes Belinda."

Benton smiled goofily, and Natasha wondered from a far-off spot in her mind if she could make her legs work. They seemed to have turned to Jell-O.

"The thing is, Belinda's breaking up with Dave," Benton confided in a low voice. He herded their small group even farther from the others. "I won't, like, pounce on her the second she does, but she's pretty, right?"

"Oh yeah, *so* pretty," Darya said flatly.

"And nice," Benton said. "She's not just pretty."

"Natasha, are you okay?" Stanley asked.

"We're leaving now," Darya said. "Bye!"

"Do you need a cup of water or something?" Stanley called after them. "If you need anything, come get me. I'm here. All right, Natasha?"

"Thanks," Darya called over her shoulder. She and Ava led Natasha past the cotton candy machine, the kettle corn stand, and booths and booths of jewelry, local artwork, and offers to have your future told.

Natasha breathed shallowly and concentrated on holding back her tears. She would never ever want to have her future told, not now.

"Sit," Darya said when they reached a picnic table by a trash can. There was half a piece of pizza caught on the rim, and Natasha felt ill.

"Not here," Natasha managed. "The snow maze."

Darya and Ava followed Natasha's gaze to the other side of the fairgrounds, where snow bricks shimmered in the sun. Mr. Bakkus must have constructed it in the middle of the night, and not many people had discovered it yet. An older man and woman stood out-side the maze when the girls arrived, but no one else.

Ava ran her finger over the domed entrance. She looked at the couple. "Are you going in?"

"Maybe later. Right now, we're just admiring," the man said.

Ava ducked into the maze, pulling Natasha behind her. Darya brought up the rear. Ava led them through twists and turns and dim passages that shimmered an unworldly gray. It was the best maze Natasha could remember. She could get lost in here. She really could.

When they reached what felt like the heart of the maze, Ava said, "How about here? Is here good?"

They sat, all three squished together with their knees drawn to their chests.

"Well, that was humiliating," Natasha said. Her voice quavered.

"Now do you agree that his motorcycle boots are stupid?" Darya said.

Natasha wasn't ready to joke about it. "He likes Belinda, and he hates poems."

"But Natasha," Ava said. She shook Natasha's knee. "Guess who *doesn't* hate poems? Guess who *doesn't* have a crush on Belinda?"

"Ha. I noticed that too," Darya said.

"Noticed what?" Natasha said.

"Stanley," Ava said.

"Totally," Darya agreed.

"Stanley totally *what*?" Natasha said.

"*He's* the one who likes you," Ava said. "Not Benton. Stanley!"

"*And* he doesn't wear stupid motorcycle boots, *and* he was the nicest of all those guys," Darya said. "Benton's fine, but Stanley's better. He couldn't keep his eyes off you, Natasha."

"No," Natasha said.

Ava nodded. "Actually, yes."

Natasha tried to rewind the scene. *Poems aren't crap*, Stanley had said. And, *Natasha, are you okay?*

"Stanley wrote the notes," Darya pronounced. "So the new question is, what are you going to do?"

Stanley, not Benton, Natasha thought. She weighed the two in her mind. *Stanley. Not Benton.* Stanley *was* nice. He said smart things in class, and, that one day, he'd told her he liked her coat.

Darya scrabbled to her feet. "My butt's cold, and if we sit here much longer, we're all going to look like we wet our pants. But you know what, Natasha?"

Natasha looked up. Darya's red hair was a halo around her.

"A boy *likes* you. Not me or Molly or Belinda or any of the other girls in Willow Hill, at least not in a crush kind of way. He likes *you*, Natasha."

"Oh," said Natasha.

"It's a good thing," Ava said.

"Is it?"

"*Yes,*" Ava and Darya said at the same time.

Ava unpretzeled herself and got to her feet. She took one of Natasha's hands, and Darya took the other.

"One, two, *three*," Darya said, and Natasha let them pull her up.

I wish boys got wishes.
Why don't boys get wishes?
Boys wish for things, too.
—STANLEY GILMER, AGE THIRTEEN

CHAPTER TWENTY

Natasha made her way back from the maze in the cover of her sisters, who stayed by her side the whole way.

Darya kept a lookout for Benton. "Though you have nothing to embarrassed about," she said.

"You can say that because you're the scary sister," Natasha said.

Darya whipped her head around and arched her eyebrows.

"Kidding," Natasha said.

"But not really," Ava said.

Darya set her jaw. "I *will* scare Benton if you want me to."

"By jumping out at him and going 'Boogity-boogity-boo'?" Natasha said.

"What?"

"Nothing. I'm just being weird. Anyway, Benton didn't do anything wrong."

"Neither did you," Ava said. She squeezed Natasha's hand. "Neither did Stanley."

"Hmmph," said Darya. Her color was high, as if she were raring for a fight. "That's true."

"Are you going to talk to him?" Ava asked.

"Not today. Today I'm just going to . . ." Her words trickled off. Was that Benton by the Slurpee machine? Was that Stanley, off to the left? It was. Stanley spotted the three sisters and lifted his hand, and Natasha turned away.

They reached Papa's booth, and Natasha gave him a tight hug. He hugged her back, startled. "Do you girls need money for lunch?" he said. "There's a hot dog stand, I think."

"Not me," Natasha said. "I'm going to wait in the truck." She hurried to the parking lot, calling over her shoulder. "I'm fine, I'm just not hungry. Sell lots of lutes!"

The weekend of the Spring Festival kicked off Willow Hill's spring break, which Natasha was glad of. No school from Monday through Friday meant no Benton from Monday through Friday, and most likely no Benton on the following Saturday or Sunday as well.

No Stanley, either.

Natasha couldn't go that long without talking to Molly, however. As soon as Molly got back from her long weekend at her aunt and uncle's, Natasha asked if she could come over.

"Sure," Molly said over the phone. "I'm grubby—do you care?"

"Not at all."

"Then I'll come right now. I'll get my mom to drop me off."

When Molly got there, Natasha launched herself at her, almost knocking Molly off her feet with the force of her hug.

"Na*ta*sha?" Molly said.

"What? Can't I hug you? Why does everyone act so surprised if I hug them?"

"You're on my toe," Molly said.

Natasha stepped backward. "Oh. Sorry."

"It is a *little* un-Natasha-like. The hugging." Molly looked at her. "Who else have you been hugging?"

"No one. Just Papa. And Darya and Ava, I guess."

"That's not very exciting."

"I know. I have something more important to tell you, anyway." She took Molly's jacket from her and tossed it into the mudroom. "Come up to my room?"

They sat facing each other on her bed, both of them cross-legged. Natasha held on to her ankles, drawing her legs in closer to her, while Molly leaned back on her palms.

"So?" Molly said.

Natasha got nervous. "First tell me about your cousin's bar mitzvah."

Molly lit up. "It was so much fun," she said. "He had to give a speech—in Hebrew! Actually, that part was boring. The best part was the party afterward."

Natasha listened as Molly described chocolate fountains and plastic blow-up saxophones and a money tree, where guests left money for her cousin, all in multiples of eighteen dollars, because eighteen was symbolic of "life," for some reason.

It sounded strange and exotic to Natasha. Then again, she supposed life in Willow Hill might sound strange and exotic to Molly's out-of-town relatives. Ancient willow trees, Wishing Days, mysterious notes—except, *ack*. Molly's out-of-town relatives wouldn't know about any of that. *Molly* didn't know about it, hardly.

Molly broke off. "Am I boring you?"

"Not at all!" Natasha said. "It sounds awesome."

"It was. And my cousin's friend was there, and he was super cute."

"Curtis?" Natasha hazarded, calling up the name from the recesses of her mind.

"Yeah!" Molly said.

"Cool," Natasha said. Her heart fluttered. "Hey, Molly?"

"Yeah?"

"You remember what you said in the cafeteria, about my having intimacy issues?"

"I apologized for that," Molly said. She uncrossed her legs and pulled her knees toward her chest.

"No, I know." Natasha took a breath. "You just . . . you might have been right, sort of."

"Meaning?"

"Meaning, you tell me all kinds of stuff about what's going on in your life."

"Because I'm full of myself? Because I'm self-centered?"

"No! Molly, just listen. This time *I'm* the one trying to apologize."

Molly's mouth fell open.

"You tell me about your life, which is great," Natasha said. "But a lot of times . . . no, *some*times, you tell me about my own life, like what I should wear or how I should do my hair or whatever."

"I do?"

Natasha nodded. "And sometimes, I guess, it makes me *not* tell you stuff. Not because I don't want to, exactly. Just . . ." She sighed. "That came out wrong. It really was supposed to be an apology."

Molly rested her chin between her knees. "My mom says I do that," she confessed. "She says I boss you around. Like, that I hand you my hairbrush and tell you to fix your ponytail, and you *do*, but my mom says it's rude of me to do that."

Natasha swallowed. "She's kind of right. I know you're just trying to help me . . . but it makes me feel dumb."

Molly was silent for several moments. "Do you know why, though? Why I give you my hairbrush?"

"Because I have bumps," Natasha said. Why would Molly point that out, when Natasha just told her it made her feel bad?

"No," Molly said. "Yes, but . . . when we were little, when we were in kindergarten, *you* always looked after *me*."

"I did?"

"Uh-huh. Even my mom says so. You're good at taking care of people, Natasha."

Natasha felt spinny. "Oh."

"But then your mom left, or whatever . . ."

Natasha snuck a glance at Molly.

"And I thought *I* should take care of *you*," she finished in a rush. "I got into the habit, I guess. And you never told me *not* to. . . . But it turns out it's been bugging you all this time! Why didn't you say something?"

"I don't know," Natasha said. "But . . . I'm saying something now—and not in a bad way, because you're right, I should have spoken up. I want to be better. I *do* want to share stuff with you."

"I want that, too," Molly whispered.

"Okay," Natasha said.

"Okay," Molly said. She gave Natasha a tremulous smile. "Is there something right now that you want to tell me? Other than how I should quit telling you what to do?"

Natasha hesitated, and then she went for it. She told Molly about the whole messy, embarrassing business: Benton, the notes, and the humiliating realization that he had a crush on Belinda, *not* Natasha.

"Oh, Natasha!" Molly said. "Why didn't you tell

me any of this *before*?" She slashed her hand through the air. "Never mind. Forget I said that. Then what happened?!"

So Natasha told Molly the Stanley part. About how Stanley did like poems, and how, at the Festival, he seemed genuinely worried when Natasha turned gray and swayed. *If you need anything, come get me*, he'd called. So maybe Stanley had left Natasha the notes? Maybe Stanley was her secret admirer?

"Of course he is!" Molly said. She bounced on the bed. "He's got to be. Na*ta*sha!"

"What?"

"What do you mean, 'what'? This is so exciting!"

"Is it? It's also pretty awful, the Benton part."

"Well. Yes. But Stanley's better than Benton any day."

"That's what Darya and Ava said."

"'Cause they're almost as smart as me," Molly said. "But the question is: What do we do next?"

"We?" Natasha asked.

Molly's eyes widened. "You! I meant you! What do *you* do next?!"

"I have no clue," Natasha said. She paused. "Will you help me figure it out?"

CHAPTER TWENTY-ONE

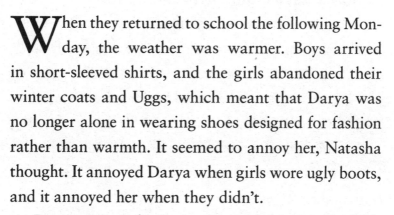

When they returned to school the following Monday, the weather was warmer. Boys arrived in short-sleeved shirts, and the girls abandoned their winter coats and Uggs, which meant that Darya was no longer alone in wearing shoes designed for fashion rather than warmth. It seemed to annoy her, Natasha thought. It annoyed Darya when girls wore ugly boots, and it annoyed her when they didn't.

But ever since the Spring Festival, Natasha had felt closer to Darya. When they got home from school after their first day back, for example, Darya brought Natasha a Coke and a plate of mini-marshmallows with peanuts stuck into them. Natasha didn't know who made up that family snack. Probably Ava. Natasha didn't like marshmallows and peanuts all that much, but it was a sweet gesture.

Ava treated Natasha more tenderly, too. She checked in with Natasha after their first day back as well, asking if Natasha had talked to Stanley and if Stanley had talked to Natasha. Was *romance* blooming in the air?

"I didn't talk to anyone," Natasha confessed. "I was too nervous. But I'm going to do better tomorrow. Molly's making me."

"She's making you?" Ava said. "How?"

Natasha took a step back from her own life. Things had been so much better between her and Molly since their talk, and Molly agreed wholeheartedly with Ava and Darya that Natasha should go for it with Stanley.

"He's so adorable," she'd said during passing period, clutching Natasha's arm as they watched Stanley make his way down the hall. "You have to talk to him, Natasha. You have to!"

But Molly wasn't *making* Natasha do anything. Natasha got to choose for herself. And, oddly, Molly's bossiness didn't bother her so much now that she'd realized that.

Molly, for her part, was trying to be less bossy. Natasha knew that. But Molly was Molly, and on Tuesday during lunch, she scooched close to Natasha and said, *"So???"*

"So what?"

Molly shoved her. Natasha laughed and said, "Ow."

"So *have you made your move?*" Molly asked. "You know that's what I meant."

"I don't have a move."

"But . . . but . . ." With sudden Molly hyperness, she took Natasha's hands and pumped them up and down. "He could be your first kiss! You could be his!"

Natasha's heart thumped. To be kissed, that was her second wish. The wish she could make happen herself. But *could* she really make that happen, her and not Molly, her and not anyone else?

"How do you know Stanley's never kissed anyone?" she asked.

"Hmm," Molly said. She held up one finger. "One sec—I'll find out!"

"Molly!" Natasha cried. "Please don't!"

"Too late!"

Molly dashed across the cafeteria, weaving through tables. Natasha couldn't watch. Five minutes later, she was back, breathless and bright-eyed. "Nope!" she said. "No kissy-kissy for Stanley, not yet. He is as unkissed as a summer's day. I asked him if he *wanted* to kiss a girl, and he said—and I quote—'It depends on the girl.'"

"Oh no," Natasha groaned.

"So I said, 'And the girl you would kiss—would her name rhyme with Flatasha, by any chance?'"

Natasha hid her face in her hands. "No. No, no, no."

"Yes! Yes, yes, yes!"

"Is he still in here? Is he watching?"

There was a pause. Then Molly pried Natasha's hands down and said, "He's gone. He's not at his table anymore. But he wants to kiss *you*, Flatasha!"

"Please don't call me that."

"Can I call Stanley 'Flanley'?"

Natasha shook her head. She loved Molly, and she was very very glad they talked more openly now. Still, she sometimes wished Molly would disappear.

Except she didn't *wish* it wish it, of course. To "wish" for something had taken on a different meaning since her Wishing Day. She was still murky on where she stood on magic—it was all so confusing! But who would wish for a person to disappear?

Natasha wouldn't wish that on anyone. Certainly not Molly.

"Well, that's boring," Molly said. "But guess what?" She put her mouth by Natasha's ear. "I told him you'd be waiting for him today after school, by the water fountain. And I picked the water fountain so you can have a quick sip of water if you get nervous, because I know how you get nervous!"

"Only when my best friend makes water fountain dates for me without my permission!" Natasha tugged a strand of her hair. "Did you honestly tell him that? That I'd meet him by the water fountain?"

"Yeppers." She clapped Natasha on the shoulder. "No need to thank me. You can just name your first baby after me."

Flolly? Natasha almost said. Instead she asked, "What did he say?"

Molly made an indignant sound. "Na*ta*sha! He said yes! Duh! And the tips of his ears turned red, which made him look even more adorkable than usual."

"Molly? I would like you to hush. Do not pass Go. Do not collect two hundred dollars. Just . . . hush."

"Will you meet Stanley by the water fountain?" Natasha sank lower in her seat.

"Will you? Promise? 'Cause think how mortified

he'll be if you don't. Can you even imagine?"

"But if I'm supposed to meet him after school . . . what am I supposed to do until then? Avoid him all day in the halls? Pretend not to see him during English class?"

Molly held up her hands and stood up from the table. "Don't shoot the messenger. Sheesh. I do think, perhaps, that *I'll* stay out of your way for the rest of the day."

"Ha, ha."

"Um, not kidding." She snaked out one arm and grabbed her sack lunch. "But will you call me after?"

"Whatever."

"Excellent. So, you and Stanley: Two-forty by the water fountain. And—oh!" She dug in her pocket and tossed Natasha a lint-covered Altoid. "They're curiously strong, you know."

"So I've heard."

Molly giggled. "You're silly. This is all going to be *awesome*, you silly, silly girl!"

Chills ran up and down Natasha's spine. She half stood, tempted to go after Molly and ask her why she'd called her that.

But Molly was gone.

During English, Natasha ignored Stanley, and Stanley pretty much did the same, although he did say hi when he passed her desk. And he smiled at her the one time she dared to look over at him. So maybe he wasn't ignoring her? Maybe he was giving her space. Or maybe he was as nervous as she was, which was pretty adorable, really.

During algebra, Natasha made a list of his charms.

1. He was nice.
2. He treated Ava like a human being, even though she was a sixth grader.
3. He had a cute best friend. (She sighed at that one, then crossed it off.)
4. He wasn't as gross as many of the seventh-grade boys.
5. He wasn't gross at all, really. He was clean and dressed nicely and didn't smell weird or sweaty or . . . weird.
6. He possibly liked poems.
7. He possibly liked her.
8. If #6 and #7 were true, then he, Stanley Gilmer, was her secret admirer.

Soon it was 2:35.

Well, she thought. She placed her hands flat on the

desk. She drummed her fingers.

I'll just peek at the water fountain and see if he's there, she thought.

She waited until everyone else had gone, and then slipped her backpack over one shoulder and tiptoed out of the room. She made sure the hall was clear. She craned her neck and peered toward the far end, where the water fountain was.

Stanley smiled at her nervously. He kinda sorta raised his hand.

Natasha ducked back and smushed her backpack against the wall.

"Natasha?" Stanley called.

Natasha took a second peek. Stanley was still there, his hand half raised and his expression puzzled. She pulled back and pressed herself harder against the painted cinder-block wall. Her backpack dug into her, so she slipped it off and held the strap with her hand.

"Natasha," Stanley said.

She heard footsteps. Oh no, was he coming toward her? She closed her eyes, as if that would do any good, and then gave up and stepped forward.

"*Oomph,*" Stanley said as they smacked into each other. Natasha dropped her backpack.

"Oh gosh, I'm so sorry," Natasha said.

"It's okay. *I'm* sorry," Stanley said.

They gazed at each other. Natasha twisted her hands.

She forced a laugh. "Molly's crazy. I mean, I love her, but she is *seriously* crazy."

"Oh," Stanley said. His face fell.

"Wait—did I say something wrong?" Natasha said. She hadn't meant to make his face fall.

"No! Just, when she asked me who I like, I guess I thought she was asking for you, maybe."

Natasha's breaths grew shallow. "She asked you who you like?"

Stanley checked both ways down the empty hall. He stepped closer. His eyes were sweet, like a little boy's. "Do you want to know?"

"Do I want to know what?"

"Who I like."

Natasha stepped backward. She no longer had her backpack on as additional padding, and she whacked her head on the wall. "Ouch."

"I hear you. I hit my head this morning. I have a lower locker."

Natasha tried to escape by scuttling sideways, like a crab.

"The girl above me?" Stanley went on, matching

her step for step. "Claire Stuber?" Two spots of red, the exact size of quarters, rose on his cheeks. "Um, she's not the girl I like. If you were wondering."

"Okay."

"But every day she leaves her locker open and talks to her friends, and every day I forget, and stand up from my locker, and *bam*."

"Ouch," Natasha said. "And you keep doing it? Day after day?"

"It's embarrassing," he admitted.

"You'd think you could just . . . remember."

"You would, wouldn't you?"

"Like, you could say to yourself, 'Stanley, *look up* before you get to your feet.'"

"And then I'd stop bonking my head. I know."

Natasha got the giggles. He was being so frank about it. "Do you really bonk your head every single day?"

"No. I might have been exaggerating."

"Good!"

"Yeah. On Saturdays and Sundays I don't bonk my head. Saturdays and Sundays are bonk-free days."

Natasha's giggles had made her feel more at ease.

"Okay . . . yes," she said.

"Yes what?"

"Yes, I want to know who you like. If you want to tell me. If you *still* want to tell me, even though you bonked your head."

"Oh. Okay, sure. Only, this time you bonked *your* head."

"I did?" Natasha lifted her hand to check. "I did. On the wall. Oh yeah." She studied him. "So we *both* bonked our heads."

Stanley rocked back and forth, hands deep in his pockets. He looked pleased. Then he stopped. He swallowed, grew serious, and said, "It's you, Natasha."

Her stomach flipped. "Me?"

"You're the girl I like."

"I am?"

"You're my favorite girl in the whole seventh grade," he said. He hesitated. "In the whole school, actually."

A huge, soundless rushing filled Natasha up.

Stanley liked her best.

Sweet, awkward Stanley, who bonked his head again and again, said she was his favorite girl in the whole school.

His *favorite*.

She would not attribute it to brain damage. She would soak it in and believe it.

221

"Are you okay with that?" Stanley asked.

"I'm okay with it," Natasha said, a smile creeping over her face.

"Really?"

"Really," she said. And since he had done something brave by telling her how he felt, she decided to do something brave in return. She rose to her tiptoes, took hold of his shoulders, and kissed him, right there in the hall.

"Wow," Stanley said when Natasha pulled back. His cheeks were redder than ever.

"Yeah," Natasha said, marveling at the world. Marveling, specifically, at the magic of unexpected things. *Good* unexpected things. *Good* magic. She didn't care where the magic came from (or if it was magic at all).

Two out of Natasha's three wishes had come true, and without anything creepy involved. Not a single corpse trying to rise from the grave, not a single beast slouching toward Bethlehem, its rough hour at hand.

Just a boy, a girl, and a kiss.

CHAPTER TWENTY-TWO

They stood there, looking at each other.

In the hall.

With nobody else around.

Natasha wanted to touch her lips, but she restrained herself. She hoped she didn't have bad breath. If she *did* have bad breath, she hoped Stanley hadn't noticed. She should have used Molly's Altoid!

It was too late now. But she really really hoped she didn't have bad breath at all.

The school clock ticked out the seconds. Above them, the fluorescent lights hummed. Farther down the hall, a bulb flickered, emitting a louder, harsher buzz. It brightened and dimmed in an unpredictable pattern. At one point, it seemed to go out entirely. Then it flared back on and burned brighter than before.

"So . . ." Natasha started. But she didn't actually have anything to say, which meant that her "so" hung in the air even after she closed her mouth. It would be there forever unless she said a real sentence. Or Stanley did. It would be nice if Stanley said *something*.

He didn't.

She didn't.

She considered an offhand remark like, "Well, this is awkward, isn't it?" But that was something a TV-show girl would say, not Natasha.

The tingles she felt earlier fizzed out. Her exhilaration at having kissed a boy—her first kiss ever—dimmed and flickered like the fluorescent light.

Shouldn't she feel different after kissing a boy for the first time ever and having him say she was his favorite girl in school? Shouldn't the feeling last longer than several seconds?

She cleared her throat. "So . . . you have good handwriting."

"I do?" he said. "Thanks. Um, you do too."

"Thanks," Natasha said, trying to recall when he

might have seen her handwriting. She'd seen his on the notes he gave her, but she hadn't written him any notes in return.

She shook her head. She needed more. "How did you get to all those places?"

"What places?"

"You know. Out by my father's workshop. The sidewalk outside your parents' store."

He looked at her funny.

"Well, I guess the one on the sidewalk wasn't that hard," she said. "But the bench at City Park? And the rope swing in our backyard?" She laughed nervously. "Do you have special invisibility powers or something?"

"Invisibility powers?" Stanley said.

Was he messing with her on purpose?

No. That wasn't Stanley.

Had an anvil fallen on his head and given him amnesia?

No. Duh. Anyway, too many locker bonks would have been more likely.

But . . . then . . . ?

"The notes you wrote," she blurted.

Natasha saw nothing but confusion in his eyes. "What notes?"

No, no, no, no, no. NOT good.

"The ones you left me. You know. You put the first one under the stone, on the path to my father's workshop. You gave me the second one that same day, when we walked to school together. It was after I tripped and everything spilled out of my backpack." She gulped. "Only I have no idea how you did it, since you were on the opposite side of the street, and since . . ."

Since the Bird Lady handed it to me, Natasha thought.

Stanley's eyes darted sideways, and Natasha's sense of self dropped straight out of her like a brick.

"Oh," she said. She tried to make her jelly legs walk backward. "You didn't write the notes."

"I could," Stanley offered anxiously. "If you want me to."

Natasha picked up her backpack. "No. Thank you, but no, and—"

She turned and ran down the hall, her shoes slapping the floor.

"Natasha?" Stanley called.

Her eyes blurred as she pushed through the heavy school doors. She ran all the way home, her breath pulling and heaving in her chest. Her heart pounded. Her legs ached.

She stopped outside the house, leaning over and propping her hands on her thighs. Her backpack dangled in front of her. She thought she might throw up. And her stupid eyes with their stupid tears . . .

Deep breaths. In through the nose, out through the mouth.

Again.

Again.

Slowly, she straightened up.

You can cry when you're in your room, she told herself. She smoothed her hair. She adjusted her shirt. She prepared a cheerful *Hi!* for her aunts, but she didn't end up using it. Her aunts weren't there.

She slipped off her shoes, cast aside her backpack, and padded upstairs in her socks. Ava's door was open, but Ava wasn't there, either. Darya's door was cracked, but not fully closed. Natasha hesitated, but a quiet approach and a peek inside told her that Darya's room was empty, too.

Huh.

Had the whole family gone somewhere without her? Well, not Papa. She'd heard sounds coming from his workshop, strings being plucked and hollow wooden knocks. Not that Papa would go out, anyway. Papa didn't go out. Papa didn't go anywhere.

227

Her gut clenched, not only because of Stanley and the notes and the kiss. Because of something bigger. Something deep and complicated and tangled up with Papa and Mama and things she didn't like to think about.

She hurried past Darya's room to her own, stopping short when she reached the door. It was closed, which would be fine if she was the one who'd closed it. But she wasn't. She clearly remembered leaving her door open that morning, because the sunlight was so buttery and not meant for secrets or small spaces or closed doors.

She heard murmurings from inside. For one long beat, she was immobile. Then she twisted the knob and burst in.

Darya and Ava turned their heads simultaneously. They were side by side on her bed, lying on their stomachs. In front of them was a notebook, spread open and filled with neat handwriting.

Her handwriting.

Her *journal*.

Her sisters.

Were reading.

Her journal.

Being angry didn't come naturally to Natasha, but

her entire body shook when she cried, "Get out! Get *out!*"

Ava scrambled to a sitting position, her eyes wide. "But Natasha—"

"*No,*" Natasha said. She strode across the room and snatched her journal.

Darya sat up and held her hands in front of her. "Okay, you're freaking out," she said, slowly and deliberately. "Yes, we read your stories. Every single one of them, right, Ava?"

Ava was pale.

"And *maybe* we shouldn't have," Darya went on. She splayed her fingers through the air in a gesture that meant nothing, but somehow conveyed that *should*s and *shouldn't*s didn't matter. "But we did, so that's that, because we can't *un*read them, can we?"

Natasha wanted to strangle her. "Get. Out." She pointed to her door. "Now."

"We will. Relax. It's not as if we're planning on living here," Darya said.

Natasha lasered Ava with her gaze, and Ava startled and scurried out of the room.

"You too," Natasha told Darya.

"Did you just *growl* at me?" Darya said. "Oh my God. Dra*m*atic." She rose from the bed and shook out her hair just so. "I *was* going to tell you something about your stories. Don't you want to know what I was going to say?"

"Not in the slightest." Spots of light swam in front of Natasha's eyes.

"Fine," Darya said. She backed toward the hall, keeping her gaze on Natasha. "I'm going to tell you anyway, though. Natasha, your stories are—"

"*Mine,*" Natasha said. "My stories are *mine*, and this is *my* room, and *my* life. *And I want you out.*"

Something flickered in Darya's eyes. Doubt? Bewilderment? Hurt?

No, because Darya didn't get hurt. And if by a fluke Natasha *had* hurt her, then great. She deserved it.

Darya lifted her chin and exited Natasha's room. At the doorframe, she turned around. "They're good. You didn't finish most of them, which was annoying, but even so, they were good. *Really* good."

Natasha slammed the door in Darya's face.

CHAPTER TWENTY-THREE

Night fell.

Natasha refused to come down to dinner.

"What am I supposed to tell Papa?" asked Ava from outside Natasha's door.

Natasha didn't answer. Papa probably wouldn't notice, anyway.

"You are in there, aren't you?" Ava said.

I don't know, Natasha said silently. *Am I?*

She knew she was being a baby, but her sisters had *read her journal*, her personal private journal. They'd read her stories, which were basically her dreams.

Ava's footsteps retreated. Minutes later, an exasperated Darya rapped on the door. "Natasha, I had to set the table *and* get everyone's drinks *and* put the bread in the basket. All of those are your jobs, and I don't like doing other people's work."

And I do? Natasha thought. They were Natasha's jobs because she was Natasha. Good old reliable Natasha. As for Darya, Natasha couldn't think of a single chore that was regularly assigned to her. How in the world had Darya managed that? How had the others let her?

On the other side of the door, Darya sighed a sigh that was very much meant to be heard. "I don't know why you're so upset. Your stories are *good*, Natasha. Is this your way of fishing for compliments?"

"Please go away," Natasha said stiffly. She closed her eyes, angry at herself for responding. Her plan had been to never talk again, and she'd failed within fifteen minutes.

And she hadn't called Molly, which she'd promised she would, because she sucked.

She sucked, her sisters sucked, life sucked.

She flung herself backward onto her bed and stared at the ceiling, which tonight also sucked.

I hate you, ceiling, she thought, and was shocked by her own venom. She amended her sentence with,

No, wait, I don't!

A memory came to her. It was summertime, and Mama and the aunts were sitting on a quilt, talking. Ava and Darya weren't there. Maybe they were back at the house with Papa. Maybe they still took naps. But Natasha was in the yard with the grown-ups, her head in Mama's lap. She remembered gazing at the sky and feeling so proud that she was having a picnic with Mama and Aunt Vera and Aunt Elena while her little sisters stayed away.

Natasha remembered little of the grown-ups' conversation, only that at some point Natasha had rolled onto her side, and Mama had scratched her back, and Mama's voice had changed from lilting to solemn, possibly even afraid. Natasha hadn't liked it, and her discomfort burned the next part of the exchange into her brain.

"'Hate' is a strong word," Mama had said. "Does anyone really deserve to be *hated*?"

"Mosquitoes," Aunt Elena said.

"The evil kings and queens in those fairy tales you're so fond of," Aunt Vera said. "The parents who kill off their children. Surely you hate them, Klara."

Mama's hand grew still on Natasha's back. Natasha wiggled, wanting the back scratch to continue.

233

"I don't think I do," she said.

"Because they're characters in a book?" Aunt Vera said with a snort.

"No, even if they were real, I don't think I would hate them," Mama had said. "I'd hate the things they did, but that's different." She'd said more, trying to explain her position, but the words had gone over Natasha's head.

Hate is a strong word had stuck with her, though. So did something else.

"We all make mistakes," Mama had said, as if she were pleading. "But isn't it possible to forgive the person, if not the action?"

"Not hardly," Aunt Vera had said with a snort. "Some mistakes are unforgivable."

Surely that wasn't where the conversation ended, but that's all Natasha remembered. That, and how quiet Mama had grown. She never did return to scratching Natasha's back.

Darya rattled Natasha's doorknob. "I'm going to sit here until you come out—unless you want me to get Papa? Do you want me to tell Papa you've locked yourself in your room like a convent?"

"Like a nun," Natasha said.

"What?"

"I think you meant . . . never mind." Natasha felt weary. "Sure, Darya. Go get Papa. We both know how that'll work out."

Natasha heard Darya slide down the door and land with a soft thump. She heard Darya shift about, maybe digging her heels in for traction, and then she heard Darya bang the door with the back of her head. The thunk of skull against wood was unmistakable.

Thunk. Thunk. Thunk. Thunk.

"Darya, quit."

Thunk. Thunk. Thunk.

"Are you kidding? Seriously?"

Thunk. Thunk. Thunk.

Natasha dragged her hand over her face. "Darya, for real. Stop banging your head on my door. *Please.*"

"Let me in"—*thunk*—"and I will." *Thunk.*

Natasha rolled onto her stomach and pulled her pillow over her head.

Thunk. Thunk. Thunk.

She pulled her other pillow over her head, along with an enormous pink stuffed dog that she got for Christmas years ago.

(*Thunk. Thunk. Thunk.*) The sound was muffled, but still there.

"Girls?" Aunt Vera called from downstairs. "What

are you doing up there?"

Natasha waited for Darya to answer. Darya kept *thunk*ing.

"Girls!"

Natasha's nerves fluttered. Had she ever failed to answer her aunt?

Thunk. Thunk. And behind the *thunk*s, Aunt Vera's footsteps on the staircase. Papa, no doubt, was sitting at the head of the table, uncertain of what he should do. Or he was still in his workshop.

The fight went out of her. She rolled off her bed and went to the door. She timed the interval between Darya's *thunk*s. She waited, and then she opened the door.

Darya fell backward into her room. "Hey!"

Aunt Vera appeared in the doorframe, puffing. "Darya, what in heaven's name are you doing?" She turned to Natasha. "Natasha, why is your sister lying on the floor?"

"I have no idea," Natasha said.

Darya scowled and pushed herself up. Her hair was mussed in the back.

Aunt Vera pursed her lips. "Downstairs, now. Dinner's on the table, and it's extremely rude to keep the rest of us waiting."

She huffed off. Natasha's and Darya's eyes met.

"She gets upset at the smallest things," Natasha said.

"*Riiight,* while you never get upset at anything," Darya said.

"You read my journal, Darya."

"Oh my God. I said I was sorry."

"Did you?"

Darya got to her feet. "There's some kind of contest in the newspaper. A writing contest, for kids. Ava thinks you should enter."

"Not going to happen," Natasha said.

Darya put her hands on her hips. "We didn't even know you wrote stories. Why didn't you tell us?" When Natasha didn't answer, she rolled her eyes and turned away.

"Hold on," Natasha said, suddenly repentant. She took Darya by her shoulders and turned her around so that they were both facing forward. With her fingers, she combed out the tangles in Darya's hair.

"Are you making me beautiful?" Darya said.

Natasha fixed one last strand. "Let's go."

After dinner, she called Molly. "I can't talk long," she said. "I have to help clean up the kitchen."

"You don't sound happy," Molly said.

Natasha paused. Her instinct to lock away painful things was strong. Also, part of her blamed Molly for setting up the whole thing. But Natasha was able to make her own decisions. She wasn't Molly's puppet. If there was anyone to blame, it was herself.

"I'm not," she confessed. Her voice grew thick, but she forced the words out. She told Molly how the afternoon turned out.

"I'm so sorry," Molly said softly.

"Me too," Natasha said.

When the night ground to an end, Natasha crawled into bed and once more gazed at the ceiling.

I do like you, ceiling, she said in her head. *It's me. I'm* the problem.

She didn't feel angry anymore. Just defeated. Also foolish, because it had taken her this long to realize that her stories mattered more to her than Stanley did. Kissing Stanley had been a letdown because Natasha hadn't really wanted to kiss Stanley in the first place.

She didn't regret it, exactly. A kiss is what she had wished for, and a kiss was what she got. *She* made it happen. Go, Natasha! But she'd realized you couldn't exchange one boy for another, just as you couldn't snap your fingers and make both of them fall in love with you, or disappear.

She sure hoped a person couldn't snap her fingers and make someone disappear.

But the truth was, she didn't have strong feelings for Stanley. She liked him, but not in a kissing kind of way. She didn't feel, like, passionate about him.

She hadn't felt passion until she caught her sisters reading her journal. She cared about her journal. She cared about her stories. But she'd wasted a wish on a kiss, because . . . she didn't even know why. Because that's what girls were supposed to want? Boyfriends and kisses and *I like you the very best*?

Magic or no magic, she could have done so much better.

CHAPTER TWENTY-FOUR

After that, Natasha ignored Stanley completely. Day after day she ignored him, because she was too embarrassed to do anything else. She acted as horribly as the evil queens and kings in Mama's fairy tales, and eventually Stanley got the hint. He stopped asking what was wrong and what could he do and was it the thing about the notes? He stopped insisting he didn't *know* anything about any notes. He stopped imploring her to explain, which was for the best since the stream of notes had dried up regardless.

Molly told Natasha she was being a jerk.

"I know," Natasha said.

"Then quit it."

"What if I can't? What if I *am* a jerk?"

"You're not. You're just acting like one."

Natasha shrugged and averted her eyes.

At home, she was cold to Ava, who didn't bug her about Stanley, but pestered her relentlessly about her stories.

"Only one of the stories had an actual ending," Ava said. "You need to finish the others."

"No thanks," Natasha replied.

"But they're *so good*," Ava said. "Like that one about the girl who turned into an owl. Did she find out why? Did she ever change back? Or was she actually an owl who turned into a girl? Because you kind of hinted that maybe she was, but then the story just ended. Only without a real ending."

"Oh well," Natasha said.

"And did Darya tell you about the young writers contest? She said she did. You should totally enter."

"Only I would rather step on a nail and have it go all the way through my foot," Natasha said.

"The deadline's May second. That's two weeks away. You could enter the shy girl story *or* the owl girl story, if you finished the owl girl story."

"Let me clarify. I would rather step on a nail, get

gangrene, and die."

"You'd rather die than enter one of your stories in a contest?"

Natasha met Ava's gaze, but there was a wall inside her that made Ava seem far away.

"Mama told stories," Natasha said. "She told fairy tales, only sometimes she changed the endings to make them better."

Ava scrunched her eyebrows together. Her T-shirt had a rainbow on it, and her barrette was plastic and yellow and shaped like a duck. Didn't Ava know that animal barrettes were for kindergartners? Didn't Ava know that she had to grow up, because there wasn't any other option?

"What do Mama's stories have to do with anything?" Ava asked.

"Just, she changed them and added happy endings, but what good did it do?" Natasha said. "She's still gone. What happened to *her* happily-ever-after?"

"Mama's not gone because she told stories."

"How do you know?"

"Because she's not. That's stupid." Tears sprang to Ava's eyes. "Natasha, why are you acting like this?"

"Like what?"

"Like . . . you're not you."

"Maybe I'm not," Natasha said. "Maybe I'm gone too."

"Natasha, stop."

"Or if I'm not gone yet, maybe I will be. Maybe I'll run away and never come back, because my sisters broke into my room and went through my stuff."

Ava's chest rose and fell. Her heart necklace, which Natasha had given her on her birthday, rose and fell too. "You're supposed to be the nice one," she whispered. "You're supposed to take care of me."

"Um, no, Mama and Papa are supposed to take care of you. I'm supposed to tell you not to wear such babyish barrettes."

Ava blanched. Then she spun on her heel and walked away.

Natasha saw her swipe her hand across her face, and she wanted to call out to her. She never meant to make Ava cry. But the wall separating Natasha from the rest of the world was still there. Could a person disappear inside herself and get really and truly stuck?

She suspected yes. A girl might *want* to stop acting awful but be unable to. A girl could be gone and not gone, at the same time.

It could happen.

Klara.

Klara.

Klara.

—Nathaniel Blok, age thirty-six

CHAPTER TWENTY-FIVE

Spring arrived for good. Aunt Vera scolded Darya for wearing such short skirts, while Aunt Elena stuck up for her, saying, "Oh, Vera. You're only young once. And Darya, you have a darling figure. If you've got it, flaunt it! That's what *I* say."

Darya shot Natasha an amused look, which Natasha did her best to ignore.

"Oh, what a *darling* figure you have," Darya whispered to Natasha as Natasha collected their breakfast dishes and took them to the sink.

At seven forty-five, when Natasha shrugged into her jean jacket, opened the front door, and promptly shrugged her jacket off because she didn't need it, Darya said, "Much better. You have such a darling figure. You need to show it off!"

"I'm not showing off my figure," Natasha protested. "It's hot, Darya."

"Oh, I *know*," Darya said.

"The weather! Not me! I don't need a jacket."

"Oh, I *know*," Darya repeated.

Natasha laughed despite herself. She, like the last icy bits of snow, had gradually thawed, and she was no longer furious at her sisters. She no longer felt trapped behind a glass wall. She didn't feel as if things were all the way back to normal, though.

"Ava?" Natasha said, her hand on the back doorknob.

Ava glanced up blankly. Then she formed her mouth into a smile. "Oh, sorry. Bye! Have a good day!"

Natasha sighed. "Thanks," she said. "You too." She vowed to smooth things out between them, today. "See you after school."

Ava wasn't at the table doing homework when Natasha came home, however. She wasn't in her room, either. When the sun began to set and Ava was still missing, Aunt Vera said, "You girls. What has gotten

248

into you these past few weeks? Has adolescence hit all three of you at once?"

Darya huffed. "I am *not* going through adolescence," she declared. "I am so past that stage."

"Good to know," Natasha said.

"Yep."

"Is that why you're only eating the marshmallows from your bowl of Lucky Charms?"

"Darya!" Aunt Vera exclaimed. "Dinner is in less than an hour! You do not need a snack less than an hour before dinner!"

"Yeah, Darya," Natasha said.

Darya stuck out her tongue, and Natasha commented on what a grown-up and mature tongue she had.

"Darya, put away the Lucky Charms," Aunt Vera said. "Natasha, go find your little sister. And Elena— really? Are you eating a bowl of Lucky Charms too?"

"Just the marshmallows," Aunt Elena protested. "Emily started it!"

Everyone looked at her. Natasha felt a shiver move through the house.

Aunt Elena laughed and smacked her forehead with her palm. "*Natasha* started it. Hunger pains are making me talk nonsense."

"Aunt Elena, I didn't start anything," Natasha said.

"Right. See? More proof that I need real food."

"Aunt Elena . . . who is Emily?"

Aunt Elena frowned.

"No one," Aunt Vera said.

"Papa said Mama had an invisible friend," Natasha said. "I mean, an imaginary friend." Her voice shook. "Was Emily Mama's imaginary friend?"

"Natasha," Aunt Elena said. She faltered. "I don't know. Truly. The name Emily . . . when I think too hard about it, I hit a blank space. And yet, sometimes that name just slips out of my mouth."

Aunt Elena turned to Aunt Vera. "Vera? Did Klara have an imaginary friend named Emily?"

"There is no Emily, there was no Emily, there never will be an Emily," Aunt Vera said. Her eyes were rabbity. "When Klara started on about Emily, that's when she . . . when she . . ."

"When she *what*?" Natasha said.

"That's when we started to lose her!" Aunt Vera cried. "She made up this *Emily*, but I don't know why, since it only distressed her. She got so worked up, insisting this Emily was real, only she wasn't!"

"I don't understand," Natasha said.

250

"We're not discussing it," Aunt Vera said. "I'm sorry, but we're not, and Elena, I'd appreciate it if you'd show more control."

"You say her name too," Aunt Elena whispered. "I'm not the only one."

"Then we'll both stop," Aunt Vera said sharply. "*We will all stop.* Understood?"

Darya rolled her eyes. Natasha pushed her chair back from the kitchen table, feeling woozy. She headed outside, and from there, across the yard. The door to Papa's workshop was cracked. Natasha knocked lightly and went in.

"Natasha," Papa said. He gave her a tired smile. "How's the . . . what is it you're studying? The civil rights movement?"

"That was last semester."

Papa nodded. "You gave a report on Rosa Parks."

"That was Darya. I did mine on Martin Luther King's 'I Have a Dream' speech."

"Ah," Papa said. "Your mother loved that speech."

Natasha felt itchy. She came out here with the intention of asking Papa about Emily, hoping he might give her an actual answer instead of snapping at everyone. But now it felt easier not to.

She scanned the room. "Have you seen Ava?"

Papa rubbed the back of his neck. "Ava," he repeated. "Let me think. I saw her this morning—or was that yesterday? Come to think of it, what day *is* today?"

"It's Friday, Papa. May second."

Friday, May second, was the deadline for the young writers contest Ava had wanted Natasha to enter. Maybe she should just enter the darn thing and make Ava happy. Except no. Duh. It was too late.

She needed to talk things out with Ava, though. She wasn't Ava's mother, but she *was* Ava's big sister. Maybe Ava felt like she needed Natasha's approval, kind of. And maybe Natasha had been withholding it. Kind of on purpose, kind of not.

"If you see Ava, tell her to go to the house," Natasha said. "It's getting close to dinnertime."

"I will," Papa said obediently.

"In about half an hour, you'll need to come in, too."

He nodded.

"We're having meatloaf," she felt compelled to add. "You like meatloaf."

"Who made it?"

"Aunt Vera, but Aunt Elena made that sauce for on top."

"The zesty sauce. Good."

He chuckled, and Natasha looked at him keenly. Nobody had called Aunt Elena's sauce "zesty sauce" in a long time. They used to joke about it, though. Didn't they?

You're horrible, Natasha remembered Aunt Elena telling Papa with a laugh. Or rather, Natasha saw the scene in her head like something from a movie: Mama, Papa, the aunts, all seated around the table. A toddler (Darya) perching proudly in a booster seat. A baby (Ava) wedged into a high chair.

Aunt Elena would have been young. She'd have been so proud of her contribution to the meal, which she would have brought from whatever tiny apartment she'd been living in at the time.

"It's called 'Meatloaf *with Zesty Sauce*,' so that's what we should call it," Aunt Elena had insisted.

Papa, impossibly tall and handsome, had said, "Out of respect. Absolutely."

"Oh, shush, Nate," Aunt Elena said, throwing her wadded-up napkin at him.

For a moment, the memory felt so real that Natasha could have sworn it happened yesterday. Then it slipped away, and she was left with an enormous sense of loss.

She had to move. She turned on her heel and strode toward the door of the workshop.

"Ava—she went to the top of Willow Hill," Papa said abruptly.

Natasha turned around. "Are you sure, Papa?"

Papa nodded. "She told me so. Said she wanted to see things from 'way up high.'"

That sounded like Ava, all right.

"Okay," Natasha said. "I'll go get her. Thanks, Papa."

The sky was the color of plums as Natasha hiked the steep, brambly path to the willow tree. She saw her first star of the night, and on autopilot she silently recited the poem Mama had taught her long ago:

> *Star light, star bright, first star I see tonight,*
> *I wish I may,*
> *I wish I might,*
> *Have this wish I wish tonight.*

She stopped there. She made no wish.

Motion caught her eye, and she turned toward the majestic weeping willow tree. Its branches were feathered with small buds, which, in the daylight, were a light, shimmering green. In the dark they looked ghostly, but beautiful.

Within the canopy of branches, Ava twirled, her arms out and her face uplifted.

Like the willow, she looked ghostly, but beautiful.

"Ava?" Natasha called out.

Ava stopped. She lowered her arms and stared at Natasha. Wind stirred the drooping branches, and Ava's hair fluttered and clung to her face. Goose bumps rose on Natasha's arms, because the breeze didn't reach her, not even the slightest whisper.

"Ava," Natasha said. She wrapped her arms around her ribs. *"Ava."*

"Oh," Ava said. She pushed through the curtain of buds and leaves and approached Natasha. A twig clung to her tangled hair. Natasha reached to pluck it out, but changed her mind. She drew her hand to her own mouth instead, parting her lips and pressing her thumb to her teeth.

"I was spinning," Ava said.

"I saw."

"I was imagining I was a fairy," she said. She paused. "You think that's dumb. I know."

"No, I don't."

255

"You do." She sounded resigned.

Natasha pressed her fingers against her brow bones and closed her eyes. When she opened them, she said, "Are you mad at me, Ava? You're mad, I can tell."

Ava brushed past Natasha and started down the hill. "We should go. That's why you came, right? To tell me it's time for dinner?"

Ava's stride was resolute. Her shoulder blades were visible beneath her T-shirt, and her hips were narrow. She was twelve years old, but the tags in her clothes said "size 10." When Natasha was twelve, she wore size fourteen.

She followed Ava, keeping a small gap between them.

"Is it that writers contest? Are you mad because I wouldn't enter it?"

Ava stopped, whirled around, and said, "I'm *mad* because you don't believe in magic anymore." Then she whirled back and started marching again.

Oh, Natasha thought as the pieces fell together. Because of the wishes, and the notes, and Stanley.

Ava cared about the contest, Natasha was sure of it. But she also wanted to believe in a world where wishes came true. Once upon a time, Natasha allowed herself to want that too. Then everything fell apart, and it was all so embarrassing and wrong and hurt so much . . .

"Ava, wait," Natasha said. She batted away a branch that Ava easily ducked under.

"It's all right," Ava said. "It doesn't matter."

"Yes, it does. Of course it does."

Ava's shoulders hunched up and down.

"I want to believe in magic," Natasha said. "I just—"

She stubbed her toe on a root that jumped out of nowhere. "*Ow,*" she said. "Seriously, Ava, will you slow down and stop barging forward like an elephant?"

"See?" Ava said. "My point exactly."

"Ava, I have no idea what you're talking about."

"You say things like how I'm an elephant, which no one else would ever say, because they wouldn't think of it. But you act like it's better to be boring and make oatmeal and stick your tongue out at your very own wishes."

Natasha's face flamed.

"That *is* what you wished for, isn't it?" Ava said, still not turning around. "To be a famous writer?"

"*No,*" Natasha said. It sounded like a lie even though it wasn't.

"Okay, whatever," Ava said. Without missing a

beat, she said, "What are we having for dinner? If it's meatloaf, I hope Aunt Elena made that yummy sauce for it."

Natasha grabbed Ava's arm. Ava shook her off. They were almost home, and the cheerful lights of the house bobbed in and out of sight as they stumbled down the winding trail.

Well, Natasha stumbled. Ava was as surefooted as a gazelle.

An elephant or a gazelle? an annoying voice inside her asked. *Oatmeal or meatloaf, tongue in or tongue out?*

"Oh, shut up," she said aloud.

Ava turned around and shot Natasha a wounded look.

"No, not you," Natasha said. "Me. I was telling myself to shut up."

Ava was already facing forward. She shook her head and didn't speak.

"Fine!" Natasha cried. She threw up her hands, and a thorn sliced the skin below her knuckles. Of course it did. "I should have entered the contest. You win. Will you please slow down?"

Ava halted abruptly. Natasha crashed into her.

"Not to be rude?" Ava said. "But I think you're the elephant."

"Ha ha." Natasha sucked the cut on her hand. Her blood was warm.

A grin split Ava's face. It transformed her. She was Natasha's sister again, not some ghost-gazelle-elephant hybrid. "I'm glad about the contest, though. Plus, it's lucky. Want to know why?"

"Why?"

"Because today's the deadline."

Natasha frowned. "Which means I missed it. How is that lucky?"

Ava looped her arm through Natasha's. The trail widened as it broke into open space, and Ava bounced forward, pulling Natasha alongside her. "It's lucky because I entered for you. Aren't I awesome?"

"Excuse me?"

"Yep!" Ava said. "I entered the story about the shy girl, since that's the only one you finished. The winner will be announced in three weeks. Are you so happy? Do you love me? Do you want to smother me with kisses?"

"No, yes, and no," Natasha said. "Ava. Did you fake all of this? All along, were you pretending to be mad just to get me to enter the contest?"

Ava thought about it. "I was mad because I was mad," she said. "I was sad, too. But I feel better now. And I'm hungry—aren't you?"

The moon lit the yard, and Natasha saw her reflection in Ava's eyes. Did Ava see herself in Natasha's eyes?

"You can hug me if you want," Ava offered.

"No thanks."

"Then I'll hug you," Ava said, and she did.

CHAPTER TWENTY-SIX

M ay was the prettiest month of the year, Natasha thought. Petunias bloomed in the window boxes Aunt Elena cared for, and downy sprigs of Carolina foxtail sprouted around Papa's workshop. It was warm enough for shorts, or, if you were Darya, cutoffs so tiny that Aunt Vera grew pinched and said, "Absolutely not, young lady."

"Oh, Vera, let it go," Aunt Elena said. "Darya, you could be a pixie, that's how cute you are."

Darya wrinkled her forehead and glanced at her outfit. *Pixie* wasn't what she was going for, Natasha was pretty sure.

Ava thrust her hand into the air and said, "Ooo! Ooo! I want to be a pixie! Can I be a pixie?"

"You bet," Aunt Elena said, which of course made Darya want to be the *only* pixie.

"No, because pixies don't wear overalls," Darya pronounced.

"Yes, they do," Ava said.

"Nope, and you're not a pixie. In fact, you're not even here at all," Darya said. She pulled her fingers into a fist, then splayed them out. "Poof. You're gone."

"Darya!" Ava complained. She turned to Aunt Elena. "Aunt Elena!"

"Ava, your sister does not have the power to make you disappear," Aunt Elena said. "And Darya, stop disappearing your sister! Do you understand?"

"Natasha's right here," Darya said, gesturing at Natasha. "I don't know what you're talking about."

"Hey!" Ava complained.

Natasha laughed.

"Such goofs, all three of you," Aunt Elena said. "Vera, were we as goofy as these girls?"

Aunt Vera scrubbed the omelet pan. "You were. Klara was." She pressed her lips together. "I certainly wasn't."

Natasha almost laughed, but then she didn't.

Vera, Klara, Elena. Three sisters, minus one.

Natasha, Darya, Ava. Three sisters. Three sisters minus one if Darya had really disappeared Ava, which made the joke a lot less funny.

Natasha couldn't imagine a life with no Ava or no Darya. Then again, there was surely a time when she couldn't imagine a life without Mama. As a five-year-old, it never would have occurred to her that a person could disappear. It shouldn't have to occur to anyone at any age, because people were important. People should be taken care of and never taken for granted. People should be . . . *honored*, just for being people.

With a jolt, Natasha realized that she'd failed miserably at that. She'd messed up big time with Stanley—A PERSON, A REAL, LIVE, NON-DISAPPEARED PERSON—and she needed to make it right.

"Finally!" Molly said during homeroom when Natasha told her. "I've been telling you and telling you—"

"I know, and you've been right this whole time. I've been such a jerk."

Molly's expression softened. "You've been *acting* like a jerk."

"So how do I make it up to him?" Natasha asked.

"Hmm," Molly said. She tapped her chin. "You could give him a stole."

"A stole?"

Molly grinned and bobbed her head.

"I don't know what a stole is," Natasha said.

"It's a scarf thing. Like, made out of dead animals."

"Right. Obviously. Well, that's not going to work for me. Also, I don't have a stole."

"You could steal a stole," Molly suggested.

Natasha groaned. "Do you have anything helpful to say?"

Molly put her hand to her heart. "Natasha. I'm hurt."

"No, you're not."

"No, I'm not," Molly agreed. "Talk to Stanley at lunch. Just tell him you're sorry." She slapped her desk. "OR, NO! Kiss him at the water fountain! Kiss him and tell him you're sorry!"

Natasha raised her eyebrows. Molly smiled hopefully, like, *Oh, come on. Aren't I cute?*

Mr. Beauprez, their homeroom teacher, breezed into the classroom and riffled through some loose papers. "All right, class, let's see what today's exciting announcements are."

Natasha tuned him out. She stayed focused on her

upcoming task. She rehearsed possible apologies, and when lunchtime came, she walked directly to the cafeteria.

As she bypassed the line for hot lunch, one of the cafeteria ladies said, "Pssst! Pssst!"

Natasha swiveled her head.

The cafeteria lady wore a broad white apron and a hairnet. There was a large mole on her left cheek. Kind of . . . *dripping off* her left cheek.

Stop looking, Natasha told herself.

The cafeteria lady banged the counter with a wooden spoon, which she then expertly flipped in her hand. She jabbed at Natasha with the handle. "*Pssst!* You, with the notes!"

Natasha drew up short. She cautiously approached the counter, and the cafeteria lady did something extraordinary. She peeled back her hairnet, as well as the hair connected to the hairnet. It was a hairnet plus wig. Underneath was no net, but a nest. With a bird in it.

Natasha's mouth fell open. She spent half a second absorbing the insanity of the situation, and then she stepped into this alternate reality. She wasn't sure she had any choice in the matter.

The cafeteria lady lowered the hairnet-plus-wig

back in place and secured it with several small adjustments. Then she curled her finger to mean, *Closer, please.* Natasha obliged. The cafeteria lady had sidled over to the far end of the lunch counter, and the other kids flowed past without appearing to notice them.

"Look," the cafeteria lady whispered. She pinched the mole on her cheek. She pulled it away from her flesh and released it. It snapped back onto her skin. It was like a puffy red clown's nose attached to elastic, only this was an elasticized mole.

"*I'm in disguise,*" the cafeteria lady loudly whispered, cupping her hand over her mouth.

"Yes, I see," Natasha said, unconsciously mimicking the cafeteria lady's too-loud whisper. The world was off-kilter. "But I have to go to lunch now. I have to sit down and eat my food."

The cafeteria lady clapped, a rapid series of pitty-pats. "Yes. Excellent. Oh, my girl, you're doing so well!"

Natasha pushed through the fog of her brain. She knew the cafeteria lady was the Bird Lady. There was no reason to play dumb. She didn't know *why* the Bird Lady was here, but she was, and wasn't there something Natasha had wanted to ask her?

"What are you doing here?" she asked.

The cafeteria lady's mouth—the Bird Lady's mouth—dropped open. "To give you the final note. What did you think?"

"Oh," Natasha said. She went cold, then hot. "Can I have it? Please?"

The Bird Lady drew herself up. "*I* don't have it."

"Then how could you give it to me?"

"Give what to you? There's no free lunch around here, you know." She cackled and waved the spoon about. "No free lunch! That's funny! Isn't that funny?"

Natasha remembered what she'd wanted to ask. The question clunked into place like a deadbolt clicking into a lock.

"Do you believe in wishes?" she asked.

The Bird Lady stopped laughing. "Of course. Don't be a numbskull."

A numbskull? The Bird Lady was calling *Natasha* a numbskull?! The Bird Lady had a bird in her hair! And a strap-on mole!

Natasha shook it off. "Did you know my mother?"

"Did I?" the Bird Lady said. "*Did* I?"

"Because one time you said you did, and that you liked her, although she was—" Natasha gulped. "A silly, silly girl."

The Bird Lady made eyes at Natasha. Then she

267

gave Natasha an exaggerated wink that Natasha had no idea how to interpret.

"It's a shame you can't ask Emily," she said. "Emily knew your mother better than anyone."

"But who is Emily?!" Natasha cried.

"Emily, Emily, Emily. It's always about Emily, isn't it?"

"No! Yes! Could you please just act normal?"

The Bird Lady shooed Natasha away with the spoon. Then she regarded the spoon approvingly. "I rather like this spoon. I think I'll keep it." She shifted her gaze to Natasha. "You would do well to do the same."

"Meaning *what*? You're telling me to steal a spoon?"

"It's better than stealing a stole, I should think."

"Stealing a . . . how do you know about that?"

"I know everything. And yes, I knew your mother, and yes, she was a numbskull too. However, no, you cannot have my spoon." She tapped the spoon against her palm. "Your wishes are what you should keep. Your wishes, your sisters, your friends . . ."

She nodded curtly. "Turn your back on them, and they might just turn their back on you."

"Ok-a-a-ay," Natasha said.

"And your friend is right. You should apologize to Studly."

Frustration coursed through her. "*Studly*? Why do you keep saying things that make no sense?"

"Studly, Stanley, Sterling." The Bird Lady waved the spoon some more. "It's the girls who matter. It's the girls who are full of magic. So do as I say, unless you want to end up like your aunt Vera." She sniffed. "Go, now. Run along. Skedaddle-y doo."

Natasha skedaddle-y did. The Bird Lady's gibberish filled up her head like cotton stuffing. She didn't know what to do with it.

See what the next minute brings, she told herself. *Just . . . hold on and see what the next minute brings, and then the next, and then the next.*

Her chest unclenched. She breathed more regularly, and the mist of impossibility lifted. When she saw Stanley eating alone, she went to him.

"Studly?" she said.

Stanley lifted his head. A blush crept over his face.

"I mean *Stanley*," Natasha said. She felt her face heat up too. She took one big breath and said, "I've been acting like a jerk, and I'm really sorry. You're my favorite boy in the whole seventh grade. It's just, I'm not ready for a relationship."

Stanley's blush deepened, and Natasha cringed. *I'm not ready for a relationship?* Where had *that* come from?

"I'm confused," Stanley said.

"Yes," Natasha said. "So am I."

"Why did you kiss me and then totally stop talking to me?"

"I don't know. I guess because I didn't know what else to do."

"Why?"

"I don't know. It was awkward. *I* was awkward. But it wasn't you, I swear."

"You *totally* stopped talking to me, Natasha."

She hugged her arms around her ribs.

"I didn't know what I'd done," he said.

Oh, this was agony. "You didn't do anything," she said.

He looked at her skeptically.

"You didn't do anything *wrong*, I mean," she said. "Somebody's been leaving me notes—well, he's stopped now—although this wacky old lady, *super* wacky, kind of said maybe there's one more? Or maybe she didn't say that at all. If you think I'm confusing, you should meet her."

"No thanks," Stanley said.

Natasha curled her toes within her shoes. "Anyway, I thought it was you who was sending the notes, but it wasn't."

He studied her.

"And even if it had been, I don't think I was ready for . . . *you* know. I do want us to be friends, though." She tried not to fidget. "It's hard to know what you really want sometimes. Do you know what I mean?"

"I thought I messed up somehow," he said.

"You didn't."

"I kept thinking, 'What did I do? What did I do?' And you wouldn't even *look* at me. It didn't feel very good, having you just . . . disappear like that."

Poof, you're gone, she thought. Shame washed over her.

"I was a jerk," she said. "If I could go back and change things, I would. I truly am sorry, and I promise I'll do better."

He made her wait. Then he wrinkled his forehead. "Why did you call me 'studly'?"

"Um . . . because you are?" she squeaked. How else could she answer?

Stanley puffed up a bit. It was adorkable.

"Huh," he said. Then, "Okay, I forgive you."

"Really?" she said. "Okay, yay! So can we be friends again?"

"Sure," he said.

"That's so great. Thanks, Stanley." Impulsively, she stuck out her hand.

Stanley looked at it—her slim hand, floating between them—then shrugged, clasped his palm to hers, and gave a firm shake.

CHAPTER TWENTY-SEVEN

Natasha dreamed it was her birthday, and that for her present, Papa made her a hot air balloon. Only it was a hot air balloon without the balloon, so it was really just a ball of hot fire. Papa gave her a ball of fire, and it scorched her, and she woke up with a start. She sat bolt upright, her heart racing. She was clutching her sheet.

It was just a dream, she told herself. *It was just. A dream.*

Usually after a bad dream, the shudder of it slipped away quickly. Usually the remnants of it seemed silly and no longer scary at all.

Not this time.

Which is why a kid needs parents, she thought. When a kid had a bad dream, a parent was supposed to show up to say "shhh" and rub the kid's back. It could be a mother or a father. It didn't matter.

Outside in the hall, she heard her sisters being hyper because it was the last day of school. She should get up and be hyper with them.

So get up! she told herself. *Up and at 'em! Last day of school! Yay!*

Ava knocked on her door and burst into her room without waiting for permission. "Natasha!" she cried. She leapt onto Natasha's bed and straddled Natasha on her hands and knees. She bounced and made the mattress rock. Her hair tickled Natasha's face.

"Guess what?" Ava said. "Guess-what-guess-what-guess-what?!"

"Ava, get off," Natasha said. She sputtered, trying to get Ava's hair out of her mouth.

Ava bounced more enthusiastically. It jostled the bad dream out of her, anyway. "I'm not going away until you guess. So guess!"

Natasha tried to push her off, but Ava was a ball of muscle. Skinny, but strong.

"Ugh, fine," she said. "Is it that today is the last day of school?"

"Nope! You lose, except actually you win anyway." She jiggled with excitement.

"Ow," Natasha said. "Ava. You're making me need to pee."

"Darya!" Ava bellowed. "She's awake! Get in here—and bring the paper!"

Natasha squirmed out from beneath Ava. She was adjusting her rumpled pajamas when Darya came in and plopped down on the edge of the bed. She thrust a section of the *Willow Hill Weekly* at Natasha.

"Look!" she said.

"At what?" Natasha groused.

"Oh, stop being a poopie and *look*," Ava commanded. She grabbed the paper from Darya and held it an inch from Natasha's eyes. "See?"

Natasha batted it away. "Hold on. Sheesh." She arranged herself in a more comfortable position and took the paper.

CONGRATULATIONS TO THE WINNERS OF THE YOUNG WRITERS CONTEST! read the headline at the top of the page.

Hope pressed hard and fast against her ribs. Her

gaze flew to Ava, whose eyes danced with excitement. Darya was playing it cool, because Darya was Darya, but she raised her eyebrows to form two pleased peaks.

Natasha skimmed the names beneath the announcement. Then she slowed down and read them again:

FIRST PLACE: ANICA RUSSO
SECOND PLACE: THOMAS BURNETT
THIRD PLACE: SKYLAR TREVARTON

Her hope came crashing down. She looked at her sisters, not understanding.

"Are you so happy?" Ava asked. "Are you so glad I entered your story for you?"

"I didn't win," Natasha said.

"Well, no, but look." Ava took the paper from Natasha, cleared her throat, and read, "'With an honorable mention to Natasha Blok.'" She lowered the paper. "That's you! You're Natasha Blok!"

"Let me see," Natasha said.

Ava handed it over and pointed to the relevant paragraph. "Read it out loud."

"But you just did."

"I didn't read *all* of it. Read the whole thing, Natasha."

Below each winner's name was a description of his or her story, with comments from the judges. And below that was Natasha's name, really and truly. There were a few sentences about her—how old she was, where she went to school, a quote from her English teacher about what promise she showed (!). Then, from the judges:

"Ms. Blok's short story demonstrates a wonderful ear for dialogue and an emotional depth far past her years. A writer to be watched."

"You're a writer to be watched!" Ava crowed.

A writer to be watched? Natasha thought. Plus she had emotional depth and a wonderful ear for dialogue. The praise made her warm. Then she wondered why, if she was a writer to be watched and those other things, did she only get an honorable mention?

She felt indignant.

Then she looked at her name, right there in the *Willow Hill Weekly.* Forget first place or second place or whatever. She was a writer. A real, live writer, and it had happened without any wishes at all.

At school, Molly gave her a huge hug.

Stanley told her how cool it was to see her name in the paper, and she said, "Thanks." She was glad they were able to look each other in the eye again.

Rameen Pezeshki said it wasn't fair that she was good at math *and* good at writing, and Belinda Berry said, "I remember that poem you wrote in fifth grade. About frogs? I'm totally not surprised your story won, because that poem rocked."

Natasha started to correct her—she didn't win, she just got an honorable mention—but ended up letting it slide. Natasha remembered her frog poem, but she had no idea anyone else did, especially Belinda, who sat on tables and flirted with boys.

She would be nicer to Belinda, Natasha decided. Just because Belinda was popular didn't mean she wasn't a possible friend.

Claire Stuber gave her a second copy of the newspaper announcement, which Claire's mother had cut out in case Natasha wanted a spare. Benton slapped her palm and said, "Keep slingin' those words, bae!"

Natasha cautiously agreed, then asked Molly what "bae" meant.

"Omigosh. That he likes you, that's all!" She blushed. "Not *like* likes you. We're done with that. And *he* should be done with the word 'bae.' But—it's his way of saying congratulations. Okay?"

"Yes ma'am," Natasha said. She couldn't suppress her grin.

Then Natasha's honorable mention got lost in the tidal wave of last-day mania. Summer! No school! Hot days and swimming pools. Popsicles, both the healthy all-fruit ones Aunt Vera bought and the decadent Häagen-Dazs ice cream bars Aunt Elena snuck into the freezer.

Papa came into closer focus in the summer, too. He came to the house more. He talked more. In the summer, Papa sometimes smiled.

Natasha was in English class, thinking about that, when a memory rose to the surface and washed over her, pulling her completely away from the real world.

"And Nate's smile," Aunt Elena had said. This was several years ago. Natasha was supposed to be in bed, but she'd come down for a glass of water. When she heard Papa's name, she paused outside the kitchen and listened.

"The way his face lit up when Klara entered the room," Aunt Elena went on. "Can't you just see it?"

"Klara made everyone light up," Aunt Vera said.

"But Nate . . . The way he looked at her . . ." Aunt Elena's tone grew wistful. "I was jealous of them—did you know that? Not in a bad way. But they were my favorite couple. They were so happy."

"Sure, until Klara up and left without a word. In

my book, that disqualifies them from the happiest couple award."

"Depression is complicated. You know that."

"Depression is a luxury."

Aunt Elena had sighed. "Not everyone's as strong as you are, Vera."

"So it's my duty to take up the slack?" Aunt Vera said. "I love those girls. I would throw myself in front of a train for them. But shouldn't that be Klara's job?"

Natasha had tiptoed back upstairs and lain in a fetal position, pulling her comforter under her chin. She wasn't thirsty anymore.

She came out of the memory and was startled by how loud her classmates were. They wore such bright colors. Their smiles were wide and easy.

When the final bell rang, the junior high students stormed the halls in a wild, hormone-driven rush toward freedom.

"Come on!" Molly urged. She pulled on Natasha's backpack. "All the seventh graders are going to Sweet Treat. The sooner we get there, the more likely we are to get seats away from Darya and her posse. Unless you want to sit with Darya and her posse?"

"I don't," Natasha said. She felt off balance. "But

you go. Tomorrow we'll spend the whole day together, 'kay?"

"Okay, bae," Molly said. She hurried to catch up with the crowd. "See ya soon, bae!"

"Love you, bae!" Natasha called.

She stood quietly for a few moments after stepping out of the school building, then started off toward home.

"Good or bad, happy or sad—at least you're not a blackbird," someone said when she was deep in the forest. "Eh? Am I right? Hmm?"

It was the Bird Lady. Natasha recognized her raspy voice.

"Where are you?" Natasha said, scanning the surroundings.

The Bird Lady popped out from behind an oak tree. She wore a long skirt today, and she swished her hips to make it flutter against her army boots. "I'm not wearing my disguise anymore."

"So I see," Natasha said. "Why'd you say at least I'm not a blackbird?"

"Oh my. What did they feed you today? Figgy pudding?" The Bird Lady joined Natasha on the path. "You can't be a *bird* because you're a *girl*."

Natasha shifted her backpack. "I know that. But you said it like I should be glad. Why should I be glad I'm not a blackbird?"

"Four and twenty blackbirds, baked in a pie," the Bird Lady said.

"Nobody is going to bake me in a pie," Natasha stated.

"Stranger things have happened," the Bird Lady said. "Haven't you learned that beneath the ordinary world lies a hidden world? The hidden world can also be good or bad, happy or sad." She nodded. "Your mother knows."

Natasha's senses went on high alert. "What?"

"I said your mother knew."

Natasha stepped closer. She smelled green saplings and blackberries and something spicy that tickled her nose.

"What do you know about my mother?"

"If I tell you, what will you give me in return?"

"I don't know. Anything you want!"

The Bird Lady's eyes narrowed. "No," she said. Her voice made Natasha shiver. "Your three wishes have been used—don't offer to give anybody 'anything' ever again. Do you promise?"

Natasha's heart pounded.

"*Do you promise?*" the Bird Lady demanded.

"Sure. Yes. Whatever."

"Your mother is gone," the Bird Lady said.

"I realize that," Natasha said sharply.

"But she left you something." The Bird Lady coyly hid her hands behind her.

"No," Natasha said. Cold sweat beaded at the small of her back. "If she left something for *me*, why would she give it to *you*?"

The Bird Lady unfolded her fingers. A note lay on her palm. It was much larger than the others, more like a letter, really, but with *Natasha* written in the now familiar handwriting.

"Do you want it?" the Bird Lady said.

Natasha's throat squeezed shut.

"As you please," the Bird Lady said, "but it's not mine." She turned over her hand, and the note fluttered to the ground.

Natasha felt faint. Her backpack listed to one side and almost tipped her over.

The Bird Lady vanished.

The note remained, two feet in front of her.

Natasha's breaths were shallow. She didn't want to

step into the air where the Bird Lady had been. She did want the note, though. She squatted and reached for it, without allowing herself to move her feet. Her fingertips grazed the paper. Her muscles strained. One more s-t-r-e-t-c-h and . . .

She had it.

I wish I could tell someone.

—EMILY

CHAPTER TWENTY-EIGHT

Natasha ducked off the path, sat on a rock, and opened the note. She read the words, fast-fast-fast. She squeezed her eyes shut and tried to empty herself of everything.

A bird sang. A small animal scuffled. A breeze ruffled the note, and Natasha smoothed it against her thighs. She looked down and read it again, each and every word:

Natasha, I saw your name in the paper! Oh, honey, an honorable mention! If I were there, I'd wrap you up in the biggest hug ever and take you out for ice cream.

I'd ask to read the story you submitted, and I hope you would let me, but if you didn't, I'd understand. Certain things are private. Certain things can't be shared, not in the ordinary way. But writing, whether you show it to anyone or not, is a safe way to let things out, isn't it?

Safer, at any rate.

You and I are alike, I think. We can both say things on paper that we can't say out loud. That's why, for me, notes are easier than talking.

That's why I got scared. I thought maybe you'd want to talk; that's why I suggested it way back when. Then I thought, "What if she's better off without me?"

The same old problem. It's always the same old problem. But that's why the notes stopped, in case you were wondering. It was me, not you. It always has been.

Oh, Natasha, you must have hated me when you read the Wishing Day letter I left for you. (You did get the letter, didn't you? Of course you did. I'm sure you did. It's just, your father . . . I hope he did as I asked, that's all.)

Well.

Sweet girl, I can't say what I need to say, out loud or on paper. I try to open my heart, and the wings come crashing down. My tears are smearing the ink.

I love you, Natasha. Always.

—Mama

When Natasha lifted her head, the forest was just as it had been. Leaves rustled. Two chickadees quarreled above her, then flew to another tree and took up their argument again. A bar of light fell across her lap, brightening the faded blue of her jeans.

Was the note truly from Mama? If it was, then the others were, too . . . right?

Natasha folded the note and tucked it into the small pouch at the top of her backpack, which she carefully zipped closed. She walked to Papa's workshop. She rapped on the wooden door.

No one responded.

"Papa?" she said.

She heard a bang, followed by a short exclamation of pain. He'd stubbed his toe, maybe, or banged his elbow on his drafting table.

"Papa, it's me. Natasha. I'm coming in."

Papa stopped nursing his thumb when she stepped through the doorway. "Natasha," he said.

Natasha thought three things in rapid succession:

He looks so old, way older than he should.

He loves me so much.

I love him, too.

Then an ache of loneliness pierced her heart. Those things *were* true, but threaded through all of them was a sadder truth:

And yet he doesn't know me, not really.

"Is it time for supper?" he asked. He squinted at the window, where dust motes floated in the gold, filmy light. "Surely it's too early for supper, unless—oh no. I didn't forget another birthday, did I?"

"Papa, stop," Natasha said. Two years ago, Ava staged an elaborate birthday dinner for Papa. She made place cards. She planned the menu. She left personalized invitations on everyone's pillow the night before, requesting that "all guests be seated in the dining room by five p.m. on the dot." It was very cute and very Ava, and at 5:01, she stepped proudly out of the kitchen with a tray of stacked blini, the Russian version of crepes.

They were delicious and buttery and warm, or they would have been if they'd been gobbled up straight away, as they were meant to be. But Ava insisted they wait for Papa, who didn't come and didn't come, and who wasn't in his workshop when Natasha pushed back her chair and went to get him. He'd gone into town because he'd run out of wood stain. He'd forgotten it was his birthday entirely.

The blini were cold and rubbery when Aunt Vera said, "For heaven's sake," and forked a bite into her mouth despite Ava's protests. The others followed suit, and everyone lied and told Ava they were perfect. Papa showed up half an hour later, baffled by everyone's chilly response.

"No, you didn't forget anyone's birthday," Natasha said, "and no, it's not time for dinner."

Papa relaxed. "Right. Yes. Good." He hesitated. "In that case . . . ?"

"Do you have a letter for me?" Natasha asked.

Papa looked at her without comprehension.

"From Mama, and you were supposed to give it to me on my Wishing Day?"

Papa rubbed the back of his neck. "Oh. That." He looked sad, like he always did when anyone mentioned Mama. "It's just that your aunts said it would be better, you see, to wait. So I held on to it."

Natasha willed herself to act calm. "But there *is* a letter? From Mama?"

"She left one for each of you girls," Papa said.

"Can I have it? The one for me?"

A shadow moved across his face. Natasha felt a swell of frustration. *Yes, be sad*, she thought. *Yes, stay in your own world. That's nothing new. But give me the letter first!*

"Papa," she said.

He pulled himself together. "Yes, yes. If Vera and Elena changed their minds, then of course." He went to the desk he used when he did his accounting. With a small gold key, he unlocked the uppermost drawer. He opened it and took out three creamy envelopes.

For all of Natasha's life, Papa's desk had stood at the far end of his workshop, and ever since she was five there'd been a locked drawer and a letter within the drawer from her mother. Three letters from her mother, and she'd known nothing about any of it.

What else didn't she know?

Papa shifted, and his broad shoulders blocked Natasha's view. She heard the drawer slide shut and the clink of the key hitting home. When he turned, he held a single envelope against his chest. He crossed the room and offered it to her, but he didn't let go when she took hold of it.

His eyes swam with tears. Seeing them made tears spring to Natasha's eyes.

"I love you very much, Natasha," Papa said.

"I love you, too," she said. She could feel the sealed flap on the underside of the envelope. On the front was Natasha's name, written in the same loopy cursive as the other notes she'd received.

"Your mother was a good woman," he said. "*Is* a good woman, and she loves you, too. You need to know that."

"Okay," Natasha said.

Papa let go of the envelope, and Natasha stumbled back. Her backpack hit a lute. Its string sighed a lonely note.

"Natasha?" he said.

"Yes?"

"Will it be dinnertime soon?" He looked old and lost, and Natasha hated him a bit, even as she loved him.

"Yes." She turned and hurried out the door.

CHAPTER TWENTY-NINE

S he went to the tree with the rope swing, but she
didn't sit on the swing. Instead, she stood on one of
the tree's big roots and looked back at Papa's workshop.
Then she looked at the house, cheerful and reassuring
in the setting sun.

The lights were on in her sisters' rooms. Darya's
blinds were shut, while Ava's curtains, gauzy and purple, were wide open. Natasha spotted Ava's feet at the
end of her bed, one on top of the other in purple socks
with yellow polka dots. Her top foot waggled back
and forth. She was probably reading a book. Probably
about magic.

Natasha shrugged off her backpack and set it by the trunk of the tree. Now she took a seat on the wooden swing. She dug the toes of her sneakers into the ground to keep from swaying.

She ran the pad of her index finger over the creamy envelope. She flipped it over, dug her thumb beneath the flap, and pulled out the letter. It was several pages long. The sheets were folded in half and creased in the middle, and when Natasha shook them open, she caught a whiff of roses.

Again, a flash of memory. A glass bottle tied with a dove-gray ribbon, and Mama saying, "You put it here, where your skin is warm," as she dabbed a drop of perfume on the inside of Natasha's wrist.

With a thudding heart, she read her mother's letter:

Dear Natasha,

If you're reading this, that means I wasn't able to fix things. Or myself. I am more sorry than you will ever know.

Oh, sweetheart.

I've started this letter a thousand times and ripped it up just as many. I can't say what I need to say. I'll never be able to say what I need to say. I have to try, though, don't I? So I'm not going to rip this one up. This is the one, because tonight will be my last night here.

Take care of your sisters and your father. No, that's not fair—you're only five, after all! You're already so accomplished, though. So smart and funny and creative, and so sure of what you want. Today you asked me to braid your hair, and you got very stern with me about the bumps. "No bumps, Mama!" you cried. "My reputation is at stake!" Papa and I laughed at that, and you got even sterner.

"Molly has bumps, and everyone in the class calls her Bumpy Molly," you informed me.

"Oh dear," I murmured, thinking about how callous children can be, even in kindergarten.

You saw my expression, and your eyes widened, and you flung your arms around me and said, "They don't, Mama! I made that up! Nobody calls her Bumpy Molly, and I just said that and I don't know why. She has the unbumpiest hair of anyone, she really really does, so change your face back, Mama. Please!"

But Natasha, I share that as an example of what an imagination you have, not to suggest you're callous. You're not callous. You couldn't be if you tried. Last week you tried to pet that mean old tomcat that lives down the road—do you remember? And he clawed you, and I was so upset. But you patted my hand and said, "Mama, shhh. Poor darling Mama. He was just having a rough day, that's all." Then you spun off into a story about all the mice you would feed him to cheer him up, but only mice that were already dead and that died of "natural causes," as you put it.

Do you still make up stories?

Do you still know Bumpy Molly, who isn't bumpy at all?

Except you're not five anymore. Maybe you wear your hair short now. Maybe you have a new best friend. (Although selfishly, I hope you don't. Molly's a good friend, and good friends are worth holding on to.)

This is awful, Natasha. I miss you already. Please just . . .

I don't know. Stay kind. Stay funny. But do be careful what you say. The world is slippery. It's easy to make mistakes, and some mistakes can't be undone.

And, yes. That's why I'm writing this. To say goodbye, to say I love you, and to warn you about your Wishing Day, which is tomorrow. If you're reading this letter, it must be, because I'm going to leave Papa specific instructions on when to give it to you. I'll be quite firm, just like you were about how you wanted your hair, you silly goose.

Thirteen years old.

Impossible.

I'll say it, then: Be careful what you wish for.

Because the old saying is true, Natasha. Do you understand? I wished for something terrible, and my wish came true. I unwished it many times over, but unwishes don't count. Although I wonder, if you wished for my wish to reverse itself, would it work? ~~Would Emily and I be best friends again?~~

Don't, darling. Never mind. Wish for chocolate cupcakes or a new dress or a patch of sunlight for that mean old tomcat. Or don't wish for anything at all!

I'm still going to try, you know. To fix the wish I wished, to be back before you know I'm gone. But the wings are beating, sweet girl. I hear them in my head, and I fear I'm losing my mind. My heart, however, is yours forever.

Love always,
Mama

The sun dipped farther below the horizon. Natasha's spine hurt from sitting so rigidly on the wooden swing. She dropped the letter to her lap and pushed at the ground, flexing her feet and pointing them to make the swing move.

She wore her hair in braids when she was little? She called Molly "Bumpy Molly," and Mama "poor darling Mama"? That sounded more like Ava than Natasha.

She didn't remember a grouchy tomcat, either. Or Emily, whose name Mama had scratched out. *Emily, Emily, Emily*, the Bird Lady had said. *It's always about Emily, isn't it?*

Everyone wanted to scratch Emily out, it seemed. Had Emily once been real? Had Emily been Mama's best friend? Had Papa and Aunt Vera scratched those memories out—or was Mama crazy?

I fear I'm losing my mind. Mama wrote those words herself.

But wait, Natasha told herself. *Go back a step and THINK, Natasha. Think what this means.*

Mama.

Is.

Alive.

A shadow caught her attention. It was Papa, standing in the window of his workshop, his hands propped against the window frame. He wasn't looking at Natasha. He wasn't looking at anything, as far as Natasha could tell.

But when he heard that he was right and that Mama *was* alive . . . !

She hopped out of the swing and ran across the lawn, tingling with the knowledge of how happy he'd be. Then she stopped. Mama was alive. Yes. But she wasn't here.

She was alive, and yet she wasn't with them, and she wasn't with them *on purpose*.

All this time, Mama could have been with them.

She could have saved Papa from his grief. She could have saved all of them from their grief.

Why did she decide to reach out now? And why why *why* did she reach out to Natasha instead of Aunt Vera or Aunt Elena, who were her very own sisters, after all? Why didn't she reach out to *Papa*, her very own husband?

Natasha swallowed and gazed at the house Mama had walked away from nearly eight long years ago. Inside the kitchen, she saw Darya setting the table, and she saw Ava following behind, straightening the knives and forks and arranging the napkins more neatly.

Aunt Vera stood at the stove, stirring soup or maybe spaghetti sauce, and Aunt Elena opened the oven and slipped in a foil-covered loaf of bread. Natasha knew what would happen next. Aunt Elena would set the timer for twenty-five minutes, and Aunt Vera would say, "Twenty-two minutes would be better. You can always leave the bread in longer, but if you leave it in too long, there's no going back."

Their routine was as predictable as clockwork, and *this*, the cheerful dance of meal preparation and easy chatter, was what defined Natasha's childhood. Maybe their family *was* broken, but in the cozy light of the kitchen, Natasha didn't see it. In the light of the kitchen, her family seemed pretty whole.

Mama was alive. (Because Natasha wished it?)

A rough beast slouched toward Bethlehem, indignant birds throwing shadows on its thick thighs. (But no, because Mama wasn't scary. Mama wasn't a *beast*.)

But maybe, in a way, Mama was *getting ready* to be reborn, only not in a scary way? (Because Mama was the one who was scared, that's what she said in her last note—the notes that had made Natasha feel so special. Maybe Natasha had called her back? Maybe all of this *was* happening, in some mysterious way,

301

because of Natasha's wishes?)

Feathers brushed Natasha's cheek, and she spun around. A nighthawk cawed and circled above her. It plummeted down, and Natasha ducked, covering her head with her arms.

"Stop it!" she cried.

The tree behind her shivered, and a flock of blackbirds took flight. Natasha was lost in a tumble of bodies and small thrumming hearts. Beaks stabbed her shoulders and her back and the bare flesh of her legs. Wings flapped noisily.

They were shooing her toward the path that led to the old willow.

"All right, all right!" she cried. Her calves burned as the trail grew steep. When she tripped, warm things kept her from falling. When she slowed down, the sting of beaks increased.

Panting, she crested Willow Hill. The birds swooped away in a tremendous flurry of wings.

The old willow tree waited. Its slender, curved branches were no longer covered with buds, but dressed in proud green leaves.

She approached. Its leafy branches rustled. *Come in, come in*, they whispered.

She pushed through the swaying curtain. Each leaf

caressed her. When she was fully within the willow's sweeping canopy, something loosened inside her.

"My mother *is* alive," she told the Bird Lady, who sat between the tree's great roots.

"Is she, now?" the Bird Lady said.

"She is. And you knew it."

"Hmm," the Bird Lady said. Her frail body rested against the willow's trunk, and her pajama bottoms were bunched over her outstretched legs. Her bunny slippers peeked from the hem. The bunny ears were white and fluffy.

She patted a spot beside her. "Come. Sit."

Natasha picked her way over and sat.

The Bird Lady searched the folds of her skirt and produced a rumpled white bag with DINO'S CANDY printed across the front. "Would you like a gummy worm?"

"No, thank you."

"I really think you should have a gummy worm."

"I don't want a gummy worm."

The Bird Lady examined her with her shiny, intelligent eyes. "Do you always get what you want?"

It felt like a trick question.

The Bird Lady opened the bag and held it out. She jiggled it.

The night could hardly get stranger, Natasha decided, so she reached into the bag and pulled out a juicy red gummy worm.

"Good," said the Bird Lady. "And now I will tell you a story."

CHAPTER THIRTY

"Once upon a time, there was a girl named Klara," the Bird Lady began.

"My mother," Natasha said.

"Klara lived here in Willow Hill," the Bird Lady went on. "She had an older sister, Vera, who was excellent at crossword puzzles and bossing people around. She had a younger sister, Elena, who liked to flatten caramels into long ropes and then roll them up to look like snails."

I know all this, Natasha almost said, but she swallowed the words. Anyway, she didn't know about the crossword puzzles. The caramel snails, yes, because

Aunt Elena still made caramel snails every so often.

"Klara also had a best friend," the Bird Lady said. She gazed at Natasha. "Do you know who your mother's best friend was? Can you guess?"

Natasha dug her fingernails into her palms. "I'd rather not."

"Hmm," the Bird Lady said.

Natasha pushed the back of her head against the willow's trunk. "Fine," she said. *"Emily."*

"Good girl."

"But is she dead? Did . . . did Mama wish her away?"

"I don't know. Did she?"

"You do so know! Because Papa talked about Emily that one time. He said Emily was Mama's invisible friend, or imaginary friend, or whatever. And Aunt Vera freaks out whenever Emily's mentioned, and Aunt Elena knows *something*, it seems like . . ."

Natasha felt ashamed. She was yelling at an old lady wearing bunny slippers. But she also felt unjustly accused. Accused of what, she couldn't say.

"Why are you so mean?" she whispered.

The Bird Lady blinked. "Mean? Am I mean?" Her expression softened. "Oh dear, I'm going about this all wrong. Don't cry, pet." She reconsidered. "Well, *do* cry if you need to. Or even if you want to. There's nothing wrong with tears."

The Bird Lady slipped her hand into Natasha's. It was a child's hand, but with wrinkles. She gave a gentle squeeze.

"Shall we start at the beginning?" she asked.

"I don't care where we start. I just want to understand!"

The Bird Lady chuckled, but not in a mean way. "Don't we all."

"*Is* my mother alive?"

"You're the one who said so, not me."

"Yes, but is she?"

"Did she tell you she was?"

"I don't know. I think so." Natasha got braver. "Because she's the one who's been leaving me notes— and you're the one who delivers them."

"Hmm," the Bird Lady said.

"She said she couldn't fix things, and I think she meant about . . . you know. Emily. Did Mama make a wish about Emily? Is that what happened?"

"Hmm."

"Okay, then please answer this, and tell the truth. Do you know Emily?"

"Hmmmmm."

Natasha exhaled. The Bird Lady withdrew her hand from Natasha's and held up one finger.

"Yes . . . and no," she said.

"Meaning what?"

"I know the idea of her," the Bird Lady said carefully.

"Okay."

"And yes, I knew her when she was a girl."

"Okay."

"But no, I don't know her now." Her words sounded like an apology. "No, I can't say that I do."

Natasha bowed her head. Mama had wished for Emily to go away, hadn't she? Or for something to happen to her. Something bad. Mama made a wish on her Wishing Day, and it had to do with Emily, who once upon a time was Mama's best friend. But now no one remembered her, except for a teeny bit.

Except . . . it wasn't so much that people didn't *remember* Emily. It was more as if Emily had been erased.

Natasha shuddered. She'd watched a horrid movie with Molly about a boy who could make anything he wanted come true. His sister said something that upset him, so in the blink of an eye, he made it so that she could no longer talk, ever. Natasha could see it in her mind, a girl with long hair, terrified eyes, and no mouth. No scar or gash where it used to be, just a slick of smooth skin below her nose and above her chin.

A mouth, and then no mouth.

Emily, and then no Emily.

What had Mama done?

"Is that why my mother left? Because Emily disappeared?"

The Bird Lady's eyes were full of sorrow.

"Because Mama made her disappear," Natasha clarified.

The Bird Lady didn't argue.

"But that would have been years and years ago. I mean, if it happened because of Mama's Wishing Day. Wouldn't it? Because Mama would have been thirteen, right? So why would she wait so long to leave? Did she just get more and more sad? Did nothing make her happy anymore, not even her . . . ?"

Natasha broke off. She put the pieces together and reeled.

"I was supposed to make it better, wasn't I?" she said. "I was supposed to read Mama's letter *before* my Wishing Day. I was supposed to wish for Emily to come back!"

"Is that what your mother told you?" the Bird Lady asked.

"No, but that's what she meant. That's what a good daughter would have done. But I messed up and everything's ruined and I can't even *tell* anyone!"

The Bird Lady raised her eyebrows.

"You know what I mean. I'm telling you, yes, but you don't count."

Her eyebrows went higher.

"Darya would think I'm crazy," Natasha said. "Molly, too—or maybe not. I don't know." She rubbed her hand over her face. "Ava would believe me, but she'd believe me too much, if that makes sense. She'd get excited and bounce up and down and want every-thing to be better *right this second*. But I'm not sure everything is going to be better. Is it?"

"I can't answer that," the Bird Lady said.

"You could if you wanted to!" Natasha cried. "I know you could!"

"If wanting something to be true was all it took, don't you think your mother would be home by now?"

Natasha fell silent. She thought about Papa and how much he wanted Mama to come home. She thought about what he would say if she told him that Mama could come home—that it was possible—but that she chose not to.

It would break his heart. It would break his heart *all the way*, into such small crumbles that it might never be able to be fixed again.

Aunt Vera and Aunt Elena couldn't know, either. What good would it do?

"It has to stay a secret, doesn't it?" Natasha said. "Mama's kept a secret all these years, about Emily. Now it's my time to keep a secret. About Mama." She searched the Bird Lady's face. "Am I right? Are you allowed to answer *that* question?"

The Bird Lady patted Natasha's leg.

"Never mind," Natasha said bleakly. "I already know the answer."

From far, far away, Natasha heard Aunt Vera's voice. It was faint and thin. She was calling Natasha in for dinner.

Natasha got to her feet and brushed herself off. Heaviness hung in her chest. "Well . . ."

The Bird Lady stayed seated. The shadows had deepened so that she blended in with the trunk. "It's going to be all right," she said.

"Is it?"

"You're a good girl."

"Am I?"

"Yes," the Bird Lady said. "And you *do* have choices, you know. We all do."

Natasha took a shaky breath.

"Natasha!" Aunt Vera called distantly. "Na*ta*sha!"

It seemed impossible that Natasha could hear her, but everything about this day seemed impossible.

"Go on, then," the Bird Lady said.

Natasha gazed up, but she couldn't see the sky. The willow branches were too thick. She gazed at the Bird Lady, but the Bird Lady was gone. Natasha frowned and touched the willow's trunk. Its bark was solid and real beneath her fingers.

She stepped away and pushed through the canopy of leaves. She walked down the steep hill. Slowly at first, but then more quickly as Aunt Vera kept calling.

"I'm coming!" she called back.

She stopped at the wooden swing, which Mama had loved. She thought for a long moment, and then she knelt by her backpack, which waited on the ground where she'd left it. She fished out a pen and a scrap of paper.

Come home, she wrote.

She folded the note into a neat square, kissed it for

luck, and wedged it into the knotted rope at the base of the swing.

Please? she added silently.

She breathed in the night air and listened to the night noises. She thought about magic. Then she slung her backpack over her shoulder and headed toward the warmth of the house.

I wish for all of it.

—THE BIRD LADY, ALWAYS

ACKNOWLEDGMENTS

Bookmaking is a magical process, and so much pixie dust was blown onto this one that I'm dazzled by its shimmer. Thank you to Edward Eager, Eleanor Estes, and E. Nesbit for cementing my conviction that what appears to be ordinary rarely is, and thanks to my parents for putting those authors' books (and so many others) into my eager little-girl hands. Thanks, too, for not being *ordinary* parents in the slightest— a compliment I extend to my entire glorious, messy family. Since this is a novel about sisters, I especially thank Susan, Mary Ellen, and Eden for being born and being awesome. Without y'all, I would neither be a sister nor know the secrets sisters share.

Thanks to everyone at HarperCollins who breathed life into this project: Kate Jackson, Susan Katz, Suzanne Murphy, Amy Ryan, Bethany Reis, Lauren Flower, Alana Whitman, Ro Romanello, Stephanie Hoover, Patty Rosati, and Molly Motch. Also, a wide-eyed and bashful thank-you to Katherine Tegen. I'm honored to have been granted passage into your world.

Thanks to Barry Goldblatt and Tricia Ready, whose magic is crazy powerful, because no way would I get the boring stuff like signing contracts and paying taxes done without y'all. Plus, you keep me afloat, and when people throw stones at me (because they sometimes do), you hug me and tell me all will be well, and then you make it so. You amaze.

Thanks to my writing buddies, especially Emily Lockhart, Sarah Mlynowski, and Bob. Good heavens, y'all keep the fairy tale alive.

Huge sloppy "thank you"s to Anica Rissi for trusting me with this box of wishes, to Alex Arnold for helping me sort them out, and to Claudia Gabel for stepping forward at the end and wrapping things up with an elegant French ribbon. I am fortunate beyond belief, and I know it.

Al, Jamie, Maya, Mirabelle, and Alisha—thanks

for being my kids and for letting me into your lives. All my best material comes from y'all.

And Randy? You are my wish come true. I love you.

When **Lauren Myracle** was thirteen, she spent hours lying on her bed, staring at the cracks on her ceiling and wishing so hard to be magic. She wanted to bend spoons with her mind, talk to her sister telepathically, and rearrange her molecules so she could walk through walls. She wanted fairies to leave gumdrops on her windowsill. She wanted well-known paths to unexpectedly lead to mystical lands and times. She also wished she would grow up to become a writer—and that part came true! (Which is not to say the other parts didn't. . . .) She's written many books for tweens and teens, including the bestselling Winnie Years series and the Flower Power series. She lives with her family in Colorado, and she thinks life is the most magical adventure of all. You can find her online at www.laurenmyracle.com.